The Executioner knew he was being followed

The men behind him weren't the most expert tails he'd ever faced. Yet he felt a prickling sensation between his shoulder blades. Somewhere along the last fifty feet of the alley, he'd have to turn and confront them. There were no other options—fight it out or talk it out, even if it gave the crack dealers a warning.

The roar of a heavy automatic surprised Bolan. It surprised the five men following him even more. They were trying to get out of the alley as the bullet struck the asphalt. One of the men screamed as the bullet ricocheted into his body.

Bolan vaulted a Dumpster, palming the Beretta as he landed. It took him a second to get his bearing and to identify the crack house. Then he spotted the silhouette of a man with a gun in a dormer window. Bolan triggered a three-round burst that knocked the man back into the attic.

The Executi_____ _____ ___ ___ ___ ___ just planned his ___ ___ ___ ___ ___ ___ scuffing on the pave___ ___ ___ ___ ___ ___ up and aimed, but ___ ___ ___ ___ ___ nander pointed at h___

"Freeze, you ___ ___ ___ ___ ___ ___ wled.

MACK BOLAN®

The Executioner

DON PENDLETON'S

THE EXECUTIONER®

FEATURING MACK BOLAN®

CAPITOL HIT

A GOLD EAGLE BOOK FROM

WORLDWIDE®

TORONTO • NEW YORK • LONDON
AMSTERDAM • PARIS • SYDNEY • HAMBURG
STOCKHOLM • ATHENS • TOKYO • MILAN
MADRID • WARSAW • BUDAPEST • AUCKLAND

First edition May 1993

ISBN 0-373-61173-0

Special thanks and acknowledgment to
Roland Green for his contribution to this work.

CAPITOL HIT

If I am able to determine the enemy's dispositions while at the same time I conceal my own, then I can concentrate and he must divide.

—Sun Tzu, 400–320 B.C.

The enemy takes false comfort in numbers. Create confusion in their ranks and the weak links will emerge.

—Mack Bolan

THE
MACK BOLAN®
LEGEND

Nothing less than a war could have fashioned the destiny of the man called Mack Bolan. Bolan earned the Executioner title in the jungle hell of Vietnam.

But this soldier also wore another name—Sergeant Mercy. He was so tagged because of the compassion he showed to wounded comrades-in-arms and Vietnamese civilians.

Mack Bolan's second tour of duty ended prematurely when he was given emergency leave to return home and bury his family, victims of the Mob. Then he declared a one-man war against the Mafia.

He confronted the Families head-on from coast to coast, and soon a hope of victory began to appear. But Bolan had broken society's every rule. That same society started gunning for this elusive warrior—to no avail.

So Bolan was offered amnesty to work within the system against terrorism. This time, as an employee of Uncle Sam, Bolan became Colonel John Phoenix. With a command center at Stony Man Farm in Virginia, he and his new allies—Able Team and Phoenix Force—waged relentless war on a new adversary: the KGB.

But when his one true love, April Rose, died at the hands of the Soviet terror machine, Bolan severed all ties with Establishment authority.

Now, after a lengthy lone-wolf struggle and much soul-searching, the Executioner has agreed to enter an "arm's-length" alliance with his government once more, reserving the right to pursue personal missions in his Everlasting War.

PROLOGUE

Mass murder came up the Potomac River in a fast boat, twenty feet of fiberglass with a 200-horsepower inboard-outboard drive. There wasn't anything unusual about the boat—on a Saturday afternoon on the Potomac.

There wasn't anything unusual about the men in it, either. By looking at them, nobody could say that they weren't three young lawyers out for some fresh air and maybe a bit of fishing on Chesapeake Bay.

Nobody could say that there was even anything suspicious about landing on the weed-grown bank by a construction site. Anybody who followed the men up the bank into the bushes, though, would have learned in his last moments of life that they weren't as innocent as they seemed.

One man unpacked powerful binoculars. A second unpacked two Uzi submachine guns, a Browning Hi-Power and extra magazines for all of them.

The third and youngest of the men started unwrapping a bundle that he'd been carrying as carefully as he would a baby. An olive-drab tube appeared, with fittings that looked remarkably like a handle, trigger and sight. The man locked the sight on top of the tube and lifted the whole assembly onto his shoulder, testing its balance.

"Feel right?" the man with the binoculars asked.

"Yeah. How long I got to run the tests?"

"Ten minutes, if the plane's on time."

"Still wish we had a second."

"Man, you think we gonna get a chance for a second shot?"

"All I'm sayin' is that I don't want the Deacon blowin' my ass away 'cause the ChiComs—"

The man with the binoculars cut him off with a menacing glare. "You got a big mouth, Julius."

"Okay. 'Cause the Deacon's *friends* can't come up with another of these babies."

"Look, Julius," the man with the guns said. "Nobody's worryin' about that second shot, 'cause they know you'll make the first one hit. How does that grab you?"

"Not much like Renée grabbin' me, but I guess that'll have to wait." Julius started the tests, and by the time they had three minutes to go he was smiling.

"All set?" the leader asked.

Julius gave a thumbs-up.

"Viets, here comes one big headache," the man with the guns muttered. Then he gave his comrades a gap-toothed grin and handed out the weapons. The leader squatted behind a bush and raised his binoculars toward the glide path of airliners approaching Washington National Airport.

The SA-7 Strela that Julius carried wasn't the latest in shoulder-fired anti-aircraft missiles. The Chinese copy was less sophisticated than the Soviet original, which was in turn inferior to the American Redeye, already obsolete.

However, it didn't matter whether a weapon was obsolete or not, if your opponent had no defense against it. One of the best ways of being defenseless against any weapon was not knowing that your opponent had it.

ABOARD FEDERAL AIRLINES Flight 621 from Miami, only a few people had ever heard of Strelas. None of them were thinking about such things. The crew was concentrating on the final approach. On weekends Washington National was hairy at the best of times. Add poor visibility, an overcrowded glide path and the single runway, and you had a pilot's nightmare.

The flight attendants strapped in for landing. So did the passengers, including Mai Binh. She was tall for a Vietnamese woman and hadn't had to tighten the seat belt much for a snug fit.

She looked around the cabin to avoid the view of the Washington suburbs unrolling below. It would never do to let the Americans know that one of the most famous actresses of the People's Republic of Vietnam was afraid of flying.

It would be even more ridiculous, considering the heroic roles she'd played in the films that her American supporters were going to be showing for the first time in their country. She'd played National Liberation Front activists, People's Army nurses, even a patriotic Vietnamese woman who flew fighters against the Americans to avenge a family destroyed by American bombs.

In fact she'd been frightened out of her wits when the B-52s flew over. Most of her neighbors and many of the soldiers had felt the same way. Even a just war was too dangerous for any sensible person not to be frightened by it.

She began to think that the Americans had lost the war rather than the Vietnamese winning it. She'd seen the size and wealth of America, and the resources it could put into something as simple as roads for people to drive to work on. Not just rich people, either; factory workers and farmers owned cars in America.

If the Americans had been willing to fight the war as hard as they produced cars—well, she wouldn't be going to Washington as she was now. And she would probably not tell her hosts about her new opinions, either. They thought the war had been horrible, which was true. They also thought that their country had been doomed to lose it. Mai Binh wasn't so sure about that.

ON THE GROUND, 20-power binoculars focused, and their holder nodded.

"Right kind of plane, right number and right time. There's our 621. Get the damned cap off that thing, Julius."

"It's been off since I finished testin'," Julius said indignantly. "Remember, this bird doesn't have an all-angles seeker head. It's strictly a tail-chaser."

"You should do real good with it, then," the gunman replied.

Julius didn't hear him. His ears were tuned to catch one sound and one only; the high-pitched squeal that would tell him the heat-seeking head of the Strela had locked on the airliner's engines.

To keep it from locking on the wrong plane in the pattern, he had to keep the head down until the last minute. He heard Calvin Pitts begin to mutter, then shut out that sound, too. If Calvin made him miss this shot, he was going to say so to the Deacon, even if it meant they both wound up in the river.

The seeker head squealed, and Julius's finger closed on the trigger. Flame spewed from the rear of the tube, then from the rear of the swiftly climbing missile.

1

Panic stalked Washington National Airport. Everyone knew there'd been a major crash. A deaf man could have felt the explosions by the ground shock. A blind man could have sensed that everyone was horrorstruck.

There were, however, at least three people who weren't on the brink of hysteria. One was the ticket agent at the Federal Airlines gate. She was calmly posting a Canceled notice over the arrival time of Flight 621. Stunned and weeping relatives of the passengers surrounded her, but they kept their distance. They seemed to know that even if the next incoming plane crashed through the ceiling onto her head, she'd finish this job before she paid attention to anything else.

The second person was a young man, with shaggy dark hair and skin that might have been either swarthy or dirty. His clothes certainly were: jeans faded almost white except for grease spots, a T-shirt that might have had a logo on it once and jogging shoes that might have been white originally.

It wasn't the young man's clothes that drew the attention of the third man. It was what he was doing. He was stalking a laptop computer left unguarded by a man in a blue three-piece suit, who now stood with his nose glued against the nearest window.

The third man had his eye on both the scruffy youth and the computer. The third man was tall, well over six feet, and moved like an athlete. His hair was dark, and his eyes were ice-cold blue.

Mack Bolan, the Executioner, studied the young man, waiting for him to make his move. Bolan hoped the guy would think twice about snatching the computer, but if he made a move the warrior would be right behind him. Airport security officers had other things on their minds right now, and so did the police and FAA.

But what Bolan had to do and what he *needed* to do were two different things. He needed a quiet moment, somewhere away from Washington National, with its panicky crowds and long lines at every public telephone. He had to make a phone call to Stony Man Farm.

Someone there would know whether Flight 621 meant a change of plans for him. He suspected his mission here in D.C. was going to be delayed, if only by the diversion of his informant's flight. Announcements of flights being diverted to Norfolk, Richmond, Baltimore, Charlottesville, Philadelphia and Albany could be heard throughout the terminal.

He also suspected that the demise of Flight 621 might draw him in before long. Airliners didn't usually shed wings and plunge to earth without something causing that kind of explosion. Instincts sharpened by the best training and many years of jungle warfare—both Asian and urban—told the Executioner that a human agency probably had some connection.

As Bolan reached that conclusion, the young man made his move. He walked casually up to the seat where the computer lay, tucked the hardware under his arm without breaking stride and headed for the gate exit.

The ticket clerk was the first to notice him. "Hey!" she called. "Stop that kid!"

Heads turned her way, including the computer owner's. He took one look at his disappearing property and broke into a run after the thief.

A small automatic pistol appeared in the thief's hand, and he fired three times. The shots almost blended together into a single sound. The computer owner cried out and clutched his thigh, then his side. The ticket clerk screamed as the third bullet punched into her terminal, but she was safely out of harm's way under the desk.

Anyone looking into Bolan's eyes at that moment would have instantly stepped out of the Executioner's way.

The warrior moved cautiously. The sight of another man running could do quite a few things, most of them bad. One was to attract the attention of the thief, who might fire again and hit another bystander. A second was to push the crowd into the kind of panic where people would be trampling and clawing one another. Bolan's life was given over to preventing that, not causing it.

He didn't even breathe rapidly as he stalked the thief along a path that carried them both out of the crowd. Screams, shouts and calls for a doctor faded behind

Bolan as he saw the thief turn into a large service stairwell.

Because of stairs leading both up and down, the area offered a good many places for ambush. Both routes also led to airport staff—more innocent people to keep out of the line of fire.

Bolan had to move quickly. No matter how fast he was, he also needed protection for the last few seconds of his rush into range.

Protection, or concealment. Just outside the door leading into the stairwell was a fire hose. Bolan picked the lock on the case and unwound the equipment. Lying prone, he thrust the hose nozzle through the door. A bullet ricocheted off the metal spout but didn't punch through.

Good. The guy was a poor shot with a small-caliber weapon. But even a small-caliber bullet could be deadly if the guy got off a lucky shot or even a safety pin could kill if that hit a vital spot. Bolan intended to deny his opponent the time to aim.

He bounced to his feet and turned the water on full blast. The hose stiffened, then leaped upward and slammed backward through the swing doors. Bolan caught the hose, tucked it under one arm and drew his Beretta 93-R from its shoulder holster with the other hand.

The solid stream of water didn't strike the thief. It did have his attention, though, as Bolan charged through the door. The thief dropped the computer, switched to a two-handed grip and fired two more shots.

They were wilder than any of the previous ones. A person's grip didn't matter as much as the mind controlling the hands. The thief's mind was seething with fear, bloodlust and confusion. By contrast no emotions distracted Bolan as his 93-R sent three 9 mm tumblers down the hall.

Off balance from the weight of the hose, the warrior shot a little high. Only one bullet struck the thief in the chest. That was enough to make him drop his pistol. The other two chopped into his throat. He stumbled backward, slumped against the wall, then slowly sank to the floor. As Bolan approached, the guy's head sagged to his bloody chest. Such a waste of a human life.

Bolan turned the valve on the hose nozzle to cut off the water, hoping it didn't ruin the computer, then moved out along the same route the thief had probably intended to use. He climbed the stairs to the next floor and continued through the service halls and storage rooms out to the airport's construction areas. The Executioner was clear.

Somebody else would eventually have a thought or two to spare from Flight 621 and might connect the dead thief and the tall dark man in the cream sports jacket and charcoal slacks. By that time, though, Bolan's trail would be too cold to be worth following.

CALVIN PITTS STOOD at the helm of the motorboat. His Uzi was slung so that no one would see it unless he was directly overhead.

If it came to that, it would be Sam Goose who took the spy out. He was in the back seat, with an Uzi across his lap. His job now was to keep a lookout.

The problem was missileman Julius. After making his superhit, he had one job: get his ass back on the boat so they could all move out. He wasn't doing it.

Pitts raised his voice. "Julius, what the hell's keeping you?"

"Lost the damned cap to the tube."

"Cap?" Goose said, resting a hand on his Uzi.

"Don't sweat about the spare parts, man," Pitts said. He tried to make his voice persuasive. He was beginning to get a bad feeling about Julius. The man sounded like he'd come down with a conscience. The only cure for that came in 9 mm pills.

"Okay," Julius said, but he wasn't moving out of the bushes, let alone down the bank to the boat.

"Julius, I'm gonna count to five. Then you're either here or you're in deep shit. One, two, three—"

On "four" Julius reappeared, but on the other side of the bushes, running and dodging. Goose leaped to his feet, the Uzi up and ready.

The submachine gun wasn't silenced, but Goose only needed five rounds. Julius's hands were thrown up and down he went.

Pitts frowned as he jumped to the bank.

"What are—" Goose began to shout after him.

But Pitts had already reached his late comrade's body and hoisted it onto his broad shoulders. Calvin was only of average height, but he was nearly as broad as he was tall, and all of his bulk was packed in muscle. To Pitts Julius was a featherweight.

The dead man's blood and Pitts's own sweat were running down his face by the time he reached the bank. "Give me a hand, Sam," he called. The gunman joined him, and they gripped Julius by the head and feet.

On a count of three they swung the body far out over the water and let him go. The corpse arced past the boat's stern, splashed into the brown-green Potomac and vanished.

"I'll go back and try scaring up the cap," Goose offered.

Pitts cut him off, raising both a hand and his Uzi. "Forget it. It don't matter if they know it was a missile that took out the plane, as long as we're not connected with the hit. Matter of fact, Deacon hopes they figure that out."

Pitts was talking fast and almost yelling. "So Julius goes in the river. When they find him, they think he's just another man who got unlucky in a drug deal. They won't think he's got shit to do with the missile, unless they see us leavin'. And the longer we stand here flappin' jaws, the more likely that is."

Goose knew when his friend was cranked up. He climbed back into the boat and sat in the stern, as Pitts took the helm.

With the throttle wide open the boat made a rooster tail as it shot up the river. Ten minutes later they passed a Coast Guard launch going the other way. But by then the guns were out of sight in a duffel bag. Five minutes after that they were docking at the marina.

It wasn't the best way to end the job, Pitts knew. Deacon Whaley was going to be moderately pissed at losing Julius, but he'd have been a sight more pissed at losing what Julius could have cost them.

MACK BOLAN SAT in a worn green armchair in an apartment on the northeast side of Washington. Night had fallen over a city that for a few days, at least, would be thinking of something besides exposing or hiding scandals, trading favors and peddling influence.

The "safehouse" was rented by the Justice Department, but if any Justice Department accountant asked why, his inquiries wouldn't get far.

The man seated across from Bolan was Hal Brognola. He took his paycheck from the Justice Department, his orders usually from the White House, and his determination to fight criminals from many years of seeing what they could do.

Brognola sipped a weak whiskey and water. "By the way, Striker, did you have any connection with a DDA thief they found at Washington National?"

"You might say we had a brief association. Not mutually profitable, though."

"No. You'll be happy to know that the computer owner is going to make it. Minus quite a lot of blood, but otherwise okay. He's well enough to complain about 'dumb cops' ruining 'irreplaceable business data.'"

"If he's alive, I suppose I can put up with being called a dumb cop," Bolan replied. "I've been called worse."

Brognola emptied his glass and noticed Bolan's expression. "Striker, you have that 'Why me, Hal?' look on your face."

"Is that what you call it? I'd call it a 'This had better be more important than the Silent Brotherhood' look. I take it you're pulling me off the original mission. If those gentlemen catch on to what the man I was going to meet this afternoon knows, he might not live much longer.''

"We picked him up at Dulles and have him under lock and key," Brognola said. "Is that enough?"

"If it isn't, am I going to get any more?"

"Yes, if I can't convince you with the facts." Brognola set his empty glass down beside Bolan's. "You know that Mai Binh went down aboard 621?"

"It was kind of hard to miss her—what, fan club?"

"Artists' Welcoming Committee."

"Whatever. They were singing old peace songs and handing out literature. Does this have anything to do with her?"

"Just this. There are rumors running around that somebody in the local Vietnamese community shot down 621 to take her out."

"What with?"

"Handheld surface-to-air missile. Now, here's where it gets bad. We have a number of visual sightings that add up to the high probability that it *was* a missile. They include both ground and air sightings. One of the air sightings was a pilot who flew C-123s in Nam. He knows an SA-7 trail like his own socks."

"How is the crash-site investigation coming?"

"You can practically walk across the Potomac on the boats they have anchored over the wreck. If anything's down there that can tell us something, they'll have it counted in a couple of days."

"You think somebody's trying to make trouble for the Viets?" Bolan asked. One probable truth, one vicious rumor and an unknown but large number of people willing to believe the worst. It added up to an ugly sum. He'd seen before what happened when that kind of deadly arithmetic was allowed to go unhindered.

Brognola nodded. "Or—and let's be honest with each other—maybe it's not a rumor."

Bolan nodded reluctantly. "There are Vietnamese who feel that strongly about Hanoi and any of its pets. Those missiles are expensive though, even on the international underground arms market. Particularly since the Russians went in for glasnost and stopped handing them out like hot dogs at the World Series."

"Want to bet that the IRA wouldn't sell one of their stockpile for the right amount? Or the Palestinians?"

"If the Viets could raise the money—"

"You have four or five grocers, liquor dealers, what have you, pooling their liquid cash. Add in one veteran we trained to use Redeyes and what do you have?"

What they had was an unpleasant picture.

"You want me to use my contacts in the Vietnamese community," Bolan stated.

"Exactly. To get at the truth, Mack, however unpleasant it might be. If the truth is that the Viets did it, we can at least try to separate the innocent from the guilty. The lynch mobs won't do that."

"And if they're innocent?"

"If the Viets are innocent, then we'll all be looking for the ones who did it."

2

"Enough, Reed."

The man Deacon Whaley was talking to nodded and left the little room in the back of the bar. The sound of reggae from a jukebox faded as he closed the door behind him. Calvin Pitts thought he heard footsteps as Reed, and maybe others, moved to stand guard outside.

He looked at the man pouring out rum on the other side of the fly-specked table. Nobody in the United States—and not many still alive in Jamaica—knew if "Deacon" was Whaley's first name, nickname or honest-to-God title.

Pitts wouldn't have bet a warm glass of Red Stripe beer that Whaley was ever any kind of minister. If he'd been inside a church except to steal something since he was baptized, Pitts would eat the rum bottle on the table.

Beyond that, he didn't let himself think too much about Whaley's past. The man couldn't read minds the way some of the men seemed to think, but he was a damned good reader of faces. If he read too much curiosity in yours, you'd soon learn that curiosity sometimes killed more than cats.

"So. How did the shootdown look from your end, Calvin?"

Whaley pushed a glass of rum across the table. Pitts picked it up and tossed it back. One had to do that, if the Deacon offered a drink. If you didn't gulp the rum you'd be in trouble; if he didn't offer you one, trouble would be an understatement.

Pitts started his report. Whaley's big round face didn't give him a single clue how it was going over, but that didn't bother Pitts. Whaley wouldn't telegraph his reaction if you came in and told him you'd just nuked the White House.

At the end of the report, Whaley poured more rum. This glass, Pitts knew, he could sip. He did, then set it down half-finished when he noticed Whaley staring at him. It was the look of a cat deciding if the mouse in front of it was worth catching or not.

"Wasting Julius was a risk."

"Not as big a one as leaving him to talk. He had the guilts real bad. I've seen them."

"So have I. More than you ever will."

Whaley's voice held hard assurance. Could he have been a clergyman somewhere along his—oh, fifty-odd years?

"I'm sure of that, boss. But I was the man on the spot. Besides, he was packin', too. He might not have waited to get to the police to make trouble. They could be fishin' me and Sam out of the river tonight instead of Julius. Don't know what you think of that idea, but I thought poorly of it then, and I think the same way now."

That was riding pretty close to the edge with the Deacon, but there was little reaction other than a slow nod.

"I can't get in the habit of second-guessing the man on the spot. Not without losing the men worth *putting* on the spot. Else I'd have to do everything myself. I can't do that and even if I could, it's not the way to go anymore."

Whaley drained his rum and continued, "There's a chance Julius was running off into the bushes to take a piss. A real small chance. So small that in your place I wouldn't have believed it either. Only thing is, we're going to have to find another missileman, and they don't grow on bushes."

Pitts said nothing.

"You were pissed at having only one shot, right?" Whaley asked.

"Not as pissed as Julius. He knew those things are cranky." He shrugged. "Guess he was as good as he said he was."

"Yeah, well, nobody's good at anything when they're where he is. You know, he used to be a fisherman back on the island. Catchin' fish every day, eatin' what he didn't sell. Now the fish—they're eatin' him. Fair's fair, right?"

"Couldn't be fairer."

Pitts wondered about the fish. He decided that any fish that could survive the pollution in the Potomac could probably digest a car battery, let alone a human corpse.

He also wondered if this was going to be a prelude to one of Whaley's long rambling stories of old times back in Jamaica. Pitts would have to listen if the boss talked, but he wasn't really in the mood. The incident on the Potomac had him wound up like a top, and he wanted a chance to come down.

Whaley pushed the rum bottle across the table to Pitts. The gunman refilled his glass. The boss nodded.

"Thing about those missiles is that today's wasn't the last one we're going to see. That means finding somebody else who can fire the things before we get the new batch."

Pitts kept his face blank. Julius had said that the missile was almost surely Chinese-built. That didn't mean the ChiComs were dealing themselves in, though. Missiles like that were all over the place. A lot of people besides the Russians could build them. A lot more could buy or steal them, then hand them over to the right people for the right price.

Pitts knew two things. One was that even if the missile-sellers didn't have some reason to hand them over cheap, Whaley still had the right amount of cash to get them. The other was that being too curious about where the missiles came from would put him in the river with Julius.

"I'll keep my ears open—"

Whaley raised a hand. "My job. Your job's doing the first hit on the Viets. We've got the rumors out now. The next thing's to make it look like some people believe the rumors."

"Tonight?"

"Any problem?"

"Not unless we're short on iron or ammo."

"No problem, man. You can have six of the boys with their personal iron, some of the M-26s and gasoline bombs, and as many M-16s and Uzis as you think you'll need. We don't have any C-4, or all the ammo we'd like for the 16s.''

Pitts ran a mental list of Whaley's gang through his mind and came up with three people who were capable of using an M-16. Automatic weapons sounded real fine, but in unprofessional hands they used up ammo like beer at a hot party.

"We'll take three 16s and make the rest Uzis. If you're goin' shoppin', think you can find us some thermite? Burns hotter than the Molotovs and sets bigger fires.''

"I'll see what Woodie's got on sale." They both laughed at the idea of Woodward and Lathrop, D.C.'s biggest department-store chain, peddling weapons and explosives.

BOLAN'S SEDAN CROSSED the Theodore Roosevelt Bridge into Arlington, Virginia, just before two o'clock in the morning. As he looked downriver he could see the blaze of lights as FAA investigators and diving crews worked on the wreckage of Flight 621.

It was late at night for anybody except night workers and night owls to be out, but D.C. had plenty of both. Most were law-abiding citizens who tended bars, watched displays in the Pentagon and stood on aching feet behind the counters of all-night grocery stores.

The others were Bolan's sworn enemies and chosen prey.

He drove as he always did, with one eye on the road and one eye watching for ambushes. He didn't expect any because the car was anonymous. But he was totally armed and ready for combat, prepared for any eventuality.

He wasn't wearing the blacksuit tonight; his mission at least began with a sit down and discussion. Nevertheless, he carried the Beretta 93-R in a shoulder holster, and a Kevlar bullet-proof vest shared space with the Beretta under the jacket. On the seat beside him was an attaché case with the 93-R shoulder stock and the .44 Magnum Desert Eagle. The rest of the case held CS grenades, flares and spare magazines.

Bolan's destination was the private dining room of the Mekong Flower restaurant in Arlington. The dining room had seen dozens of Arlington's Vietnamese immigrants baptized, married and buried, as well as a number of ordinary parties.

It also held the monthly meetings of the White Tiger Society. Publicly a fraternal organization for Vietnamese businessmen, it was actually a collection of Vietnamese veterans determined to hasten the day when their homeland would be free.

The White Tigers weren't the only contact Bolan had in the Vietnamese community, but they were one he had by himself, without any help from Brognola or anybody else in the government. They would talk to him because they remembered Sergeant Mercy *and* the Executioner. They might even talk freely enough for Bolan to begin and end his mission tonight.

For two minutes Bolan allowed himself to be optimistic. Then he turned off Route 66 and began his zigzag approach to the Mekong Flower, through the dark streets of Arlington's Vietnamese neighborhoods.

Vo Le made his way up one aisle of the store and down the other, checking the windows and back door as he went. Nothing seemed to be wrong, and he turned off all the lights except the security ones.

Then he let himself out the front door, locked it and pulled the already half-drawn security shutters the rest of the way closed. Americans, he understood, complained of having to be so careful. They should have tried to run a shop in Saigon.

Le walked down the street, keeping to the lighted areas. The gangs were bad, but so far none of his children or those of his deceased brother had fallen in with them. Phu wanted to join the Army, and Le knew that his sister-in-law wasn't entirely happy about that.

Had Phu been listening too much to the White Tigers, or more likely, their sons? Many of them talked of going into the Army, to train themselves for the war of liberation. Perhaps they were right. They were certainly young enough that they might see it.

Le's generation, however, wouldn't live that long. They'd made their choice and would live and die here in the new country they'd chosen. The best they could do was to live and die honorably, with pride both in what they'd been and in what they'd since become.

Le decided to stop off at the Mekong Flower. The back room would still be open, and tonight wasn't the night for a White Tiger meeting. He would telephone his assistant to open the store in the morning, have a drink or two, and if any White Tigers came in—

His plans for the night and for everything else ended in the next moment. So did his life. What ended it was a 9 mm bullet, fired into Le's chest from a CZ-85 automatic in a long-fingered Jamaican hand.

The assassin waited until he saw that Le was down and not moving, then signaled to the men waiting behind him in the shadows of the alley.

ONE DOWN, Calvin Pitts noted. Not old enough to be called a papa-san, but definitely a grown man.

Good. The Deacon's orders about women and kids were specific, and Pitts didn't want to have to roust somebody this early into the job.

With automatic weapons and grenades there would undoubtedly be bullets and bits flying all over everywhere and hitting anybody who wasn't down flat or behind something solid. That was okay with Pitts, because it was okay with the Deacon.

"We don't want the avengers of Flight 621 to look like wimps," Whaley had said, just before the hit team left. "Women and kids went down on the plane. So taking out a few women and kids won't piss off the newspapers so much."

"It'll piss off the Viets, though."

"*Precisely,* man. So pissed that they won't think before they hit back. And 'cause they won't think, they'll hit some women and kids, too. Then everybody'll be on everybody's ass until the riots of 1968 look like a pizza party."

"Everybody's ass except ours."

Now Pitts signaled the man with the CZ-85 to cross the street. He waited until there was no traffic at either intersection, then moved. The alley on the other side swallowed him up.

Pitts waited a minute to see if anyone responded, then crossed the street into the alley, drawing his Browning Hi-Power as he went. The two remaining men had .38s; one carried a Mini M-14 and the other an Uzi.

The man with the CZ-85 unslung his other weapon, one of the three M-16s. Four of the six hitters were in position on the street. The other two, with the van and the other 16s, would be along in a minute to block the west end of the street.

Then the four already in position would start leap-frogging up the street, alternately shooting and covering one another, while tossing grenades where it looked like they'd do some good. Two minutes should be enough to chop up the whole street, along with anybody who didn't haul ass out the back of the stores.

Pitts gave the team on the far side a minute, then waved them the "get ready" signal. As he did, the blue Dodge van pulled into the intersection and stopped. The streetlighting let Pitts see the windows cranking down and two M-16s sticking out.

It also let him see a dark-colored Buick come roaring out of the night and rear end the van.

BOLAN HADN'T SUSPECTED the van of anything more than drunk driving until it stopped. Even then his first thought was to wiggle the Buick around the corner and keep his appointment at the Mekong Flower. The Arlington police could take care of the van.

Then the vehicle's windows sprouted M-16s, and Bolan knew he had a problem. Or rather the Vietnamese on the street had a problem.

The Executioner had a solution. In fact he *was* the solution.

First stage of the solution was to give the men in the van something to think about. Best weapon for that— the Buick itself. Bolan's foot hit the accelerator.

The van was heavier than the Buick, and the car didn't have much room to pick up speed. It still hit hard enough to make the van bounce, then fall back. One of the doors popped open, and a rifleman fell out. He was big, black, and not very pleased with whoever had rammed the van.

He also held on to his M-16. By the time Bolan had unbuckled and slipped out of the driver's side of the Buick, the rifle was pointing his way. A flurry of 5.56 mm rounds pierced the car's body, and shattered glass sprayed the seats of the car and the pavement.

Except for a few chips of glass, nothing came close to the Executioner. Undistracted as well as unhurt, he raised the Big .44 Desert Eagle in both hands and fired.

Two .44 slugs punched into the rifleman's chest. One would have been enough to kill. Two made his chest virtually explode.

Bolan fired another round into the rear of the van, to make sure its gas tank was good and leaky. Then he sprinted for the rear of the Mekong Flower.

If anybody was planning anything serious, there had to be more gunners around than the two in the van. From the roof of the Mekong Flower, Bolan had a better chance of seeing them. He might not be able to hit them, unless he managed to borrow one of those M-16s, but he might be able to prevent them from joining forces with the gunners in the van.

If he could do that, it would give the civilians along the street time to clear out. Then it would be a straight fight between the Executioner and the gunmen. So far that kind of fight had gone Bolan's way.

Bolan hit the alley at a dead run and leaped for the Mekong Flower's fire escape without breaking stride. He caught the last step, and the ladder came down with a hideous squeal, louder than the collision or the gunfire.

A man's head popped out of a dirty window almost in Bolan's face. He looked Vietnamese. Bolan switched to that language.

"Enemies in the street. Everybody must get out the back doors. It's too dangerous to stay. Spread the word."

"Who are you?"

"A soldier, fighting your enemies."

The head popped back inside and the window slammed down. Bolan heard shouts as the man raised the alarm inside. He kept climbing up the three flights of the fire escape to the roof.

3

Calvin Pitts was beginning to get a very bad feeling about this hit.

First the Buick took out the van, and there went half the wheels. Then one of his people got wasted—too far away to see whom it was, but that meant one M-16 out. Nobody in sight who could have done it, either. Pitts didn't believe in hexes, but he was beginning to believe in some fairly high-class opposition.

He was sure about that when he heard the voice shouting warnings from the window of the building. It sure sounded like a warning, even if Pitts couldn't understand a word.

Worst of all, the three survivors from the van were bunched up at the far end of the street. A great target for the Viets if any of them were packing.

Pitts wished he had a radio, even if it meant the police listening in and learning what was going down. He signaled the team across the street to start leapfrogging. If he couldn't radio the van team, the next best thing was to start grenading storefronts. They couldn't miss that, and if they had any brains left at all....

The first grenade blew a dry cleaner's front window halfway down the street and started a fire among clothes hanging behind the counter. Pitts grinned.

When that fire reached the cleaning solvents, everyone would have to take notice.

He slapped his number-two man. "Cover me," he ordered and pulled the pin on a grenade.

As STOREFRONTS STARTED to disintegrate, Bolan realized he had to do two things fast. One was to draw the fleeing Viets toward him, so that he could stay between them and the gang. The other was to keep the gang divided. A single party could coordinate better than two. Seven coordinated men was pretty stiff odds, even for the Executioner.

As it stood, he could probably take down most of them, but not without civilian casualties or packing it in himself by allowing the gang to get too close. Bolan knew that he might have to go out that way sooner or later, but his instincts told him that tonight wasn't the time.

A moment later experience told him that there was a better way. The gunners near the van were the key. Once they were down, the gang would lose most of its long-range firepower. In the meantime there was the problem of the civilians.

Another storefront blew out as Bolan pitched a CS grenade down the alley, toward the far end of the street. A second flew after it. The gas swirled up, eerie and dim in the shadowed alley. It would keep any Viets from running back toward the oncoming gang. It should also keep the hardmen from coming through to take the Viets from the rear.

If there was an alley on the other side of the street, it was out of Bolan's throwing range. He ran back to the fire escape. Rusty iron clanged and squealed as his feet touched the first step. Vietnamese were swarming out of buildings all along both sides of the alley. A quick look told him that they were swarming his way, and that able-bodied adults were helping the older people and children.

The noise from the fire escape alerted an armed Vietnamese that here was an enemy. A bullet ricocheted off the fire escape railing. Bolan decided that this was no time to stay and argue. He vaulted the railing, caught himself with both hands and swung feet-first through the nearest window.

Sash splintered and glass shattered. The Executioner felt wood and glass gouge his skin as he came through the smashed window. Somebody in a corner of the room let off a shotgun blast that blew out the glass Bolan hadn't demolished.

In an instant the warrior closed in on the shotgunner, wrestled the weapon out of his hand and punched him sharply on the jaw. He hoped the man wasn't hurt, but he couldn't afford to have either the gun or its trigger-happy owner behind him. The shotgun had a sling, and the warrior hung the weapon across his shoulder before he went on.

He stalked through the other rooms on the second floor of the Mekong Flower. At any front window he was in pistol range of the van. The three men behind it were harder to make out. The Executioner saw a shiny pool of leaked gasoline surrounding the van and spreading halfway along the Buick.

Bolan showed himself briefly in the window. An M-16 gunner fixed his position and shot off a whole magazine in one burst. Plaster, paint and glass rained down on Bolan as he dived out onto the balcony.

The Beretta coughed out a 3-round burst, the slugs ricocheting along the pavement, striking sparks. Some of the sparks reached the gasoline.

Fumes hadn't accumulated, so the gasoline went up with an orange *whoosh* rather than with a bang, which drove the men behind the van out into the open. Bolan dropped one of them with the .44, but he wasn't in range to target the other two quickly enough.

In the next moment it didn't make any difference. There were plenty of fumes in the gas lines of both the Buick and the van. They exploded, and so did the Buick's tank.

Bolan felt the balcony sway under him and heard chunks of cornice and roofing crash onto the balcony and the street below. If any windows on the street had survived the grenading so far, this last explosion finished them for sure.

A warrior's reflexes hurled Bolan's body into action. He hung on to his weapons, vaulted the balcony railing, felt it tear loose from the wall as he dropped and rolled clear as he struck the pavement. This brought him out into sight of the other hitters farther down the street, as several whistling bullets told him.

They also told him that the other half of the gang was too shaken by the explosion, or too afraid of hitting their friends to shoot well. Bolan squeezed off two 3-round bursts from the Beretta to make sure their nerves wouldn't improve soon. Then he ran in a crouch across the street, making a half-circle behind the wall of flame and around the two vehicles.

"GODDAMN SON OF A BITCH!" Pitts swore. Four men, all with clear shots at the guy and not a single hit!

He stopped swearing when he realized his partner was glaring at him. If they started drawing down on one another now, they'd have had it for tonight and maybe for good. The Deacon might forgive failure or even stupidity. He didn't forgive breaking discipline.

Besides, Pitts's own hand wasn't too steady. He really shouldn't be trashing anybody else's shooting.

"Sorry," he said. "This guy's not just good, he's lucky. Let's run his luck out." He motioned his partner forward and crouched to cover him.

If luck was playing fair tonight, the other side was now trying to get to the men from the van. Three against one ought to keep the opposition busy while the rest of Pitts's men closed in.

Pitts heard the stutter of an Uzi coming from behind the flaming vehicles. Somebody had a good start. Maybe they could take down the opposition and waste a few more Viets before they had to haul ass.

Just then, Pitts's partner jumped into the air, arms outstretched as if he were trying to fly. He came down on his knees and twisted so that Pitts could see his face—or what was left of it.

Pitts wanted to puke. Then he did puke, because the next gun he heard was an M-16, and it was putting more bullets into his dead partner.

He had the sense to pull back out of sight of whoever was behind the M-16. It was all he could do, because his stomach demanded his undivided attention.

The hitter knelt in a narrow air shaft between two stores, retching and heaving. There he was safe from the other side's gunfire and from having to hear his people dying.

THE EXECUTIONER DIDN'T blindside the three men behind the burning vehicles, but he did the next best thing. They'd separated, maybe at the first explosion, and out of mutual supporting distance. Two had moved right, one left. The man who'd gone to the left carried an Uzi.

He was crouching behind a mailbox as Bolan approached. The box prevented either man from getting a clear shot at each other. It didn't slow Bolan's advance or prevent the man from raising his Uzi. The warrior moved faster than his opponent. He wouldn't have had to if he'd simply wanted a clear shot with the Beretta. But the Executioner wanted a silent kill or better still, a prisoner. Either way he intended to give no warning to the other two men.

The man with the Uzi was a professional. He controlled both his surprise and the stuttergun's tendency to rise. The first burst passed mere inches above the Executioner's head. The second would have blown it off, if it had been fired.

Instead the man was slammed back against the steel box, propelled by two hundred-odd pounds of muscle, bone and controlled fury. His head cracked like an egg, and the Uzi tumbled from twitching hands into Bolan's firm ones.

The kill wasn't totally silent, but the two men were in no position to do anything about the Executioner. One was heading out to the flank—not a bad move, except that the second man was now between him and Bolan. The second man had an M-16 and might have had time to use it—against anyone but the Executioner.

Bolan shot him, ducked behind the box and hit the ground as the last man's bullets ripped into it. The shot from Big Thunder was almost trick shooting, fit for a carnival sideshow.

Only the trick was on the last hitter, because Bolan fired from where the man wasn't expecting him. Also, the .44 Magnum round could take a man out even if it only hit him in the ankle.

Bolan's shot not only hit the man's ankle, it nearly blew off his foot. He was down and screaming when the warrior popped up. He tried to draw his holdout gun but wasn't quick enough to beat the Executioner. The warrior slammed his foot on the man's arm, then popped him in the mouth, ending his screaming without ending his life.

The Executioner took a moment to turn the man's belt into a tourniquet, so he wouldn't bleed to death from his mangled foot. Then he checked the M-16 and its ammunition supply. A lot of criminals seemed to think that automatic weapons were magic wands, and never thought of minor details like ammunition. This was handy for people like Bolan when they faced such criminals, less so when they needed to borrow a weapon and found that it was out of ammo.

The grenade explosions had stopped, and Bolan didn't hear any shooting from up the street. He also didn't hear any screams. Good. That might mean no civilians near the line of fire.

Bolan slammed a fresh magazine into the M-16 and shifted position.

The remaining men down the street seemed to have frozen. That gave Bolan the initiative as long as they stayed frozen and he was free to move. He decided to wait, though, to see if any of them made targets of themselves.

As long as everybody stayed put, it was a standoff. He might even be able to pin them down long enough for the police to arrive. Police restrictions on lethal force and due process might leave the men alive, but they'd be out of circulation for a while. Unless they were crazy enough to open up on the police. In that case...

Now that he'd wiped out half the gang, it didn't matter if the two separated forces joined up. There was nothing for the survivors to join except several corpses and a cripple. Bolan could afford to leave them free to move for a bit, while he tried to get behind them.

The two men to the warrior's right must have been afraid of the same thing. They ducked back through a store and burst out into the alley less than fifty feet ahead of Bolan, whose arm snapped up and over, sending two CS grenades down the alley. Both spewed gas, raising a silvery-gray cloud that neatly blocked the alley.

One of the men ran back the way he'd come, not even trying to shoot. Bolan didn't waste a bullet on him, because the other man dived for cover behind a garbage Dumpster.

Bolan threw his last grenade, rolling it along the top of the Dumpster so that it must have dropped almost on the lurking man's head. Unfortunately the grenade didn't go off.

The Executioner flattened against a dirt-scabbed brick wall as the man rose from cover to throw the grenade back. That was a mistake. In doing so he gave the Executioner a much better target than the warrior needed.

The man ducked back down too fast for Bolan to make a body shot. He had to go for the head. Nine millimeters weren't the massive slugs of the Desert Eagle, but a 3-round burst did a fine job of shattering the man's skull from the eyebrows on up.

Bolan's eyes started to burn, and his nose felt as though he had the early stages of a bad cold. He realized that a trace of breeze was blowing the CS gas toward him.

Time to get out of the alley. Nothing was left but a body count, and he could leave that to either the Viets or the police.

Bolan kept close to the wall and kept an eye on his back. He was almost out of the alley and almost clear of the gas when he heard someone shout in Vietnamese.

"Stop! Drop your guns and raise your hands!"

THE MAN WHO CAME across the street toward Calvin Pitts was Sam Goose. He was coughing and wheezing, and looked about as pale as anybody that dark could be.

Pitts knew what they both would look like if he and Sammy didn't haul ass. They'd look like a couple of fresh corpses.

"We're movin' out," Pitts said.

"Just like that?"

"Well, you don't have to come. You can stay and get wasted."

"Lead, man. Don't jaw."

Pitts led. He didn't risk trying to get back to their car. The big guy might not be on their trail, but it was a safe bet that some of the Viets had pulled up their socks, grabbed guns and hit the streets.

The only good thing that might come of that was if some of the Viets drew down on the police. Then they would be in it real deep. That's just what Deacon Whaley wanted. If that didn't happen, there wasn't going to be a whole big load to show for tonight's fight and the loss of six men.

Pitts shivered in spite of the heat of the summer night. The last time any of Whaley's top men got a bunch of his soldiers wasted, he took it personally. He took the *men* out personally, too.

There wasn't a hell of a lot Pitts could do about it if that was what the Deacon decided to do again. But maybe he could argue the Deacon into doing something else. Like letting him set a trap for the big guy who'd messed things up tonight.

Yeah, that might work. It damned well better work, because Pitts knew one thing about the trap. If Deacon let him set it at all, Mama Pitts's boy Calvin was going to be the main bait.

"I'M A FRIEND to the people of this street," Bolan said.

His voice was steady. The problem was being loud enough to be heard, but not so loud as to sound menacing. He knew that a lot of nervous civilian fingers were tight on triggers at the end of the street, and probably more elsewhere that he couldn't see.

He counted seven weapons in front of him, from cheap automatics up to Colt .45s. They looked too large for the slightly built Vietnamese, and if even one of those fingers got any more nervous, the Executioner was going to be history.

"You have Tho's gun," a voice said accusingly. "How did you come by it, without being the man who struck him?"

"Is he dead?" Bolan had pulled his punch as much as he could, but if the man had fallen the wrong way...

"No. His head is too thick for that," someone else said, which got a few laughs.

"His head was also too thick to tell a friend from an enemy," Bolan said. "This was no shame for him, for we were both hurrying. But if you look at this gun you'll see that he fired one shot. If he had aimed a little lower, I'd be dead and six men I killed or captured would be alive to kill many of you."

Keeping his hands in full view, Bolan unslung the shotgun, put it down, then pushed it with a toe toward the mob. An older man walked forward, picked it up and scuttled back to safety as if the pavement had caught fire behind him.

Bolan knew he wasn't out of danger yet. "I'll tell you where to find the men I captured," he said. "Send armed men to each of those places, and you'll know that I'm telling the truth about why I came here tonight."

This suggestion touched off a lively debate, with most of the Vietnamese speaking faster than Bolan could accurately follow. He understood the general drift of the conversation, which leaned toward giving him the benefit of the doubt.

He hoped they'd do more than that. He needed to be out of the area before the police arrived.

Somebody came up to the rear of the crowd, asked politely to be let through and got no results. The man's tone sharpened.

A stocky middle-aged man strode through the crowd. He had a Ruger Blackhawk in his belt and a grim look on his face. He marched up to Bolan, then turned his back on the big man.

With his body shielding his hands from view, he made the secret sign of the White Tiger Society. Bolan kept his face straight and tapped the countersign on the man's left wrist.

Without turning, the stocky man said, "This man was invited here on the business of the White Tiger Society. When he says that he is a friend he speaks the truth. Now go and do as he told you, or the prisoners will escape. If they do, *you* will be telling the police why."

The idea of trouble with the police—on top of everything else—got the crowd moving. The stocky man started to follow.

"Wait," Bolan said. He handed the M-16 to the man. "Some of the drug men were killed with this. You'll need it to make the police believe that it was your fight."

"What about fingerprints—" the man began, then nodded as Bolan held up his black-gloved hands. In one of them was a business card. The man took it.

"Call that number if the police make trouble for you."

"Will it reach you?"

"It'll reach someone who always knows where I am. Tell the White Tiger Society that my business with them isn't yet finished. They'll see me again."

"If evil men— These were of the drug gangs, weren't they?"

"I believe so."

"If men of the drug gangs die whenever we see you, we hope to see much of you."

"Not without a price."

"And what is that price?"

For a moment Bolan thought he was going to have to get down to a full-scale bargaining session, here in a dark Arlington alley with police sirens growing louder in the distance.

Then the stocky man shook his head. "No, I see you have no price except honor. We won't take any of that away from you. I promise."

"I accept your promise," Bolan said, as formally as he could manage. His voice was still under control, but his feet were beginning to itch.

"Good. Then we shall meet again."

Bolan made it out of the area, which the police had cordoned off, with a couple of minutes to spare. The police didn't know exactly what they were looking for, even though they'd brought a SWAT team along to help them out.

This helped Bolan. Unfortunately it also helped Calvin Pitts and Sam Goose to escape five minutes earlier in the opposite direction. And by the time the police began to figure out just what they had on their hands, any possibility of combing the Virginia suburbs for possible fugitives was already gone.

4

"Jamaicans."

"Are you sure?" Bolan asked.

Brognola shrugged. "The immigration files on the legals gave us some IDs. The accents match, and one guy admitted to being from Kingston."

It made sense to Bolan. The Washington area had acquired a large Jamaican population in the last generation. Some of the Jamaicans had taken over a large share of the area's prosperous drug trade. Their methods, morals and tactics would have made even a Colombian drug lord frown.

"Too bad you didn't get the leader," Brognola added. "We'd have a better idea of who sent them and why. The Weatherby would have been handy there."

A ghost of a smile touched the warrior's lips. "Hal, if I took everything I *might* need every time I went anywhere, I'd be a better target than a fighter. Besides, the local police get nervous when they see a man carting around a sniper rifle less than ten miles from the White House."

"I suppose you're right."

"Back to our Jamaicans," Bolan said. He looked toward the window. A yellow, hazy dawn was creeping across Washington, promising another muggy day.

"We don't have a firm 'why.' Do we have a reasonably firm 'who'?"

"Deacon Whaley has to be in the circuit somewhere," Brognola said. "The IDs are firm for two men we know were his. The rest could have been new members, or free-lancers hired for the job."

"Or sent over to help Whaley by another Jamaican boss," Bolan suggested.

Brognola frowned, and the warrior could see that the big Fed didn't like the thought. The Jamaicans had a reputation for vicious turf fights. These confrontations killed a lot of people, but most of them weren't innocents. The fights also kept the Jamaican drug gangs divided. If the gangs were beginning to cooperate...

"I'll have Aaron Kurtzman run that idea past the computers," Brognola said. "I hope to God it isn't true, though."

"So do I." Bolan got up and poured himself a glass of ice water from the motel room's modest wet bar. "But it never pays to assume the bad guys are stupid just because it makes our jobs easier.

"So, do you have any ideas for the next step? If you don't, I'm going to visit our friend Whaley."

"I can't see how Whaley serves any real purpose in the great scheme of things. But keep the Viets out of it. I've had the White Tiger Society offering volunteers, and the police are deeply concerned about vigilantes. I've kept the Viets out of hot water so far. But if they go into Jamaican turf looking for payback, my hands will be tied."

Bolan started to ask who would tie them, then decided he probably already knew. If the White Tigers had any official connections, they were linked to the CIA. That meant the rest of the national intelligence establishment wouldn't touch them.

The President himself could save the White Tigers, but only at the price of starting a brawl in the national intelligence establishment. He'd probably think that too high a price for saving a few hotheaded Vietnamese.

In the President's position, Bolan would probably have thought the same thing.

Bolan drank more water. The heat of the day coming was already beginning to wrestle with the room's ancient air conditioner. "I'll need an ammo resupply and all the hard data you have on Whaley's base, if he has one. If not, I'll pick out one of his operations and start with it."

That cut their chances of taking out Whaley himself, but any of his operations would have its own garrison. Wipe out a few more of his hired guns, and Whaley would have a morale problem on his hands.

"You can have anything you want up to an F-15 Strike Eagle," Brognola said, "on one condition."

"Yeah?"

"Talk to the White Tigers. I think they go deaf when I come on the phone. They owe you at least a polite hearing."

DEACON WHALEY FROWNED as King Harris popped the top off a bottle of beer and chugged half of it. Frown was all he could afford to do. He thought Harris drank too much, but he needed the man's cooperation.

For now. Harris was getting older, lazier and drunker. His contacts, however, made him the best man for springing a trap on the man who'd wreaked havoc on Pitts's operation the previous night. And while he was working with him, Whaley would also be learning more about his gang.

There had to be a young lieutenant in Harris's ranks, ready to accept Whaley's help in taking over. Then, a few months later, Whaley could reel in Harris's whole gang, turf and all.

If the lieutenant didn't fight it, he might even be allowed to live. Live, and be groomed as a replacement for Calvin Pitts, if he messed up once too often.

Harris's sixth beer vanished as fast as the first five. When it was empty, Harris wiped his mouth and mustache with the back of his hand and nodded.

"I can do it. Any organization you want me to mention, just to make things scarier?"

"Try the Silent Brotherhood."

"Man, they scare *me!*"

The Silent Brotherhood was a small but ruthless right-wing terrorist organization. Their plans for nonwhites made Hitler look almost civilized.

So far they'd stayed on their home turf in the Pacific Northwest, but Whaley knew that they were trying to expand their operations. It would be easy to spread a rumor that the man who'd defended the Viets last night was a Silent Brotherhood agent.

"We got to get people real scared, King. Don't get them scared enough, and they stop to think. Then where'd be we?"

Harris made an obscene gesture. "I can have things set up for tomorrow, maybe tonight. Anything else I can help you with?"

"You make enough noise about the Silent Brotherhood, and I'll owe you more than you've ever dreamed anyone was going to pay you. I take losing six of my people kind of personal, or didn't you notice?"

After the sixth beer Harris probably wouldn't have noticed if he was being squeezed to death by a snake. Whaley suspected it was more than the beer that was making his companion mellow. It was the idea of having Deacon Whaley, the top man in Washington's Jamaican drug scene, in his debt.

"No. You don't lose people and forget it. Not you. Not me. We're two of a kind."

They might be two of a kind, but that didn't mean King Harris was going to learn about anything else Whaley had in the works over the next couple of days. He especially wasn't going to learn about another trap for the big man. That was going to be Pitts's chance to clean up his record.

Over in Anacostia, Whaley had been running a little action for a couple of months. Before dawn he'd put out the word that he was turning it into a big operation, with Pitts at the helm.

It wasn't the safest thing to do, because Anacostia wasn't his turf. It wasn't absolutely anybody else's, either. Nobody should move in on Pitts before the man they wanted heard about it. Then, when he came in, they'd be ready for him.

"WE MUST SEND SOMEONE with you," the stocky Vietnamese said.

Mack Bolan looked around the dirty alley. Nobody on the street at either end of the block was paying any attention to them, nor was anybody close enough to recognize them. If people saw them at all, they probably would assume the men were engaged in a drug deal. Like quite a lot of northeast Washington, it was that kind of neighborhood.

"It would be wise if you didn't," Bolan said. "The police will see anyone who comes with me."

"Not if you're as good a soldier as you were last night," the Vietnamese said. "We'll send only men who are good enough to stay hidden. They, too, will avenge our dead."

"Then the police will know that you have such men, and they won't trust you."

"It is known why we keep soldiers, and the police won't complain."

That was closer to boasting of the White Tigers' CIA connection than Bolan thought wise. The CIA wasn't supposed to operate inside the U.S. It tried not to let the rule tie its hands too much, but sometimes it had no choice. Such as when somebody stepped in it and the media or the FBI found out.

If the White Tigers talked out of turn and got caught in that feud, the CIA would dump them faster than an empty beer can. Bolan didn't want that to happen. They were brave men whose only faults were a touchy sense of honor and a belief that their adopted country needed them more than it really did.

At least Brognola's orders left Bolan some discretion. Then again, the big Fed never gave any other kind. He himself had too often been the man on the scene with his hands tied by the ignorant orders of distant superiors.

"How many men must you send?" Bolan asked.

The Vietnamese smiled thinly. "If I can choose the man, one will be enough."

"Will he be ready tonight, able to take care of himself, willing to obey my orders and stay out of sight?"

"You ask much."

"I know enough of the White Tiger Society to believe that I don't ask more than it can give."

The flattery drew another thin smile. "One man, then. He'll bring his own weapons, so you need not concern yourself with that."

CIA-supplied weapons, undoubtedly. If a ballistics lab traced a bullet in some Jamaican corpse to such a weapon, there would be hell to pay. But one problem at a time.

It took them nearly ten more minutes to settle the details. By then Bolan was sweating in the airless alley. It reminded him too much of Saigon.

"Our man will be there as you wish," the Vietnamese said. "Now go in prosperity and victory, until we meet again."

Bolan went. He found the street outside the alley even hotter, being in the direct early-afternoon sunlight. It was also just as humid and almost as airless.

The warrior took an evasive route to the nearest Metro stop in case anyone was tailing him. Nine times out of ten nobody was, but every so often the tenth time revealed not merely a tail but a would-be hitter.

Bolan knew that the White Tiger Society wanted one of their men along not only to avenge Vietnamese honor. They also wanted to see if Bolan was really on their side. If he had stonewalled the stocky Vietnamese, the White Tiger Society wouldn't have cooperated at all.

The man had to know who Bolan was, even though he was using the alias of Rance Pollock. So why the testing, and why the distrust?

Bolan suspected he'd have to know who the Vietnamese was before he could even guess that. He was going to learn, too, whether the man liked it or not. Somebody very high up in the White Tiger Society might be known only to people very high up in the CIA. But Hal Brognola had people up there who owed him favors. He also had Stony Man Farm's own impressive files.

The Executioner would accept a partner for tonight's battle. Before the next battle, however, he would know who this Vietnamese was.

THE BRICK DUPLEX in Anacostia was on a hill overlooking the District. The building showed signs of being partially renovated, and rumor had it that somebody had been attempting to turn it into a halfway house for teenaged girls, some runaways, some pregnant. Then they ran out of money to finish the job and couldn't find a buyer. That was until Deacon Whaley spread a little money in the right places.

Calvin Pitts looked out the attic window at the broiling street, slanting downhill toward the left. He wouldn't have minded finding a few teenaged girls in the house, instead of a bunch of empty paint cans and rickety stepladders.

It had been quite a while since he had a woman, and it would be quite a while longer before he got another one. Deacon Whaley had made that clear.

"You think you got time for chasing, go ahead and chase. But if the man we're after gets away again because you were chasing, you're in it real deep. Deep, like Julius."

Sam Goose came up the stairs with his catfooted gait and almost caught Pitts by surprise. He'd nearly drawn before he recognized the man.

"How's it going?"

"Damned near everything's unpacked, and the first van's already left."

"Everything" included a small arsenal, with more M-16s and ammunition to burn, and a not-so-small supply of crack. "No reason we can't cut some real deals while we're waiting," Goose said.

"Anybody make us yet?"

"Nobody for sure. But there's a couple kids playin' stickball across the street."

"You said a couple kids. Any particular kind?"

"Well, one of them looks a lot like somebody who runs with the Black Crabs. Courier, school dealer, stuff like that."

The first time Pitts had heard of twelve-year-old boys running drugs, he hadn't liked it. Then he understood that it was a lot harder for the police to suspect a kid, let alone put him out of business. Since Pitts liked being in jail even less than he liked getting kids in trouble, he stopped worrying.

The Black Crabs weren't as easy to erase from his mind. Nobody had Anacostia buttoned down, but the

Black Crabs had more operations running here than anybody else.

"Think the Crabs could have promoted him?"

"Could be. Want I should go out and whomp his little ass?"

"Sure, man, and tell everybody we're on to him. Better hold it until he whistles up somebody we can talk to in the Crabs."

"Then what?"

"Then we talk, man. We tell the Crabs why we're here and what we want to do. We even cut them in on the dealing. If they help us take out our target. You remember the man, Sam. No such thing as too many guns, when somebody like that's comin' down on you."

BOLAN CROSSED the Anacostia River over the 11th Street Bridge at twilight. The air smelled of the thunderstorms the radio had been predicting. To the west clouds were already building up.

The Executioner drove an elderly Pontiac, as anonymous as the previous night's Buick. Nobody would suspect that the vehicle held anything worth stealing, let alone a rifle squad's worth of firepower.

Bolan was tempted to let the other man in the Pontiac help him wield that firepower. Sergeant Chuyen had served in both the ARVN Rangers and the elite Black Panther Division. He was a good soldier by the standards of any army. Making him an observer offended Bolan's tactical instincts. They were telling him loud and clear to use every resource at hand.

Chuyen had met Bolan that afternoon, shortly after Hal Brognola's courier delivered the intelligence report on the night's target. The sergeant either didn't speak much English or was hiding his knowledge of it. Bolan's Vietnamese was enough for the briefing.

"This place is new. Suppose it's a trap? Vietcong places like it were, many times."

"These people aren't as good as the Vietcong. Also, they don't know that we are coming."

Chuyen grimaced. He knew that in Vietnam security had been the biggest problem in any operation. VC sympathizers or talkative ARVNs could blow secrecy within hours.

"They won't learn it from me," Chuyen said, and began field-stripping his weapons for a final check. He had one of the previous night's captured M-16s and a Ruger Security Six. He had five magazines for the assault rifle and a whole box for the Ruger.

The Executioner had his three standards—the 93-R, the Weatherby, and the Desert Eagle—plus grenades, mostly CS and thermite. He wore a blacksuit, and in the trunk of the Pontiac were masks and gloves for both men.

They didn't mask up until Bolan parked the car some distance from the target. By then, time and the oncoming storm had turned twilight to darkness. The streets were well-lighted, but the few people outside seemed in a hurry, eager to get out of the rain or maybe to avoid being spotted.

The Weatherby went across Bolan's back, the .44 Desert Eagle rode on his hip and the 93-R was leathered in a shoulder holster. In the shadow of a sagging back porch Chuyen locked and loaded his M-16. Then, at a nod from Bolan, the Vietnamese fell back, letting the Executioner take point.

BEFORE DINNER Pitts suspected that the trap was a bad idea. By the time it got dark he was sure.

Too damned many people seemed to be watching the house. Not all of them were kids, either. Some of them might want to buy, which was okay, but the others were pretty sure to be reporting to someone. This wasn't a neighborhood where you hung around on a summer night just because you were curious about the new people moving into the house across the street.

They had a little bit of luck, though. One of the streetlights was out, leaving a dark patch where a man could sneak across the street.

Pitts tossed the last take-out container into a corner and wiped his mouth. "I'm going to sneak over to that vacant lot and see what's comin' through there," he said. "Don't anybody sweat, unless I'm not back in ten minutes."

"Hey, man, you don't have to make like Rambo," Goose protested. The other four men nodded. Pitts wanted to think that they liked him, but he knew better. If he got wasted, then it would be *their* turn for trouble from the Deacon if it really hit the fan.

On the other hand, if he just sat on his butt while the Black Crabs got ready to blow it away, he'd be smarter not waiting for Deacon. Head over to Rock Creek Park and jump off that high bridge, the one people used when they wanted to off themselves—it would be a lot quicker.

Pitts took his Browning Hi-Power; no point in hassle from some teenaged mugger. In three minutes he'd used an alley, the shadow and another alley to get in position. He stopped, because he didn't need to go any farther to answer his questions. What he needed was to get back to the house and get ready for a fight.

Sitting in the darkness at the rear of the vacant lot were four hard-looking young Jamaicans and a fifth who wasn't so young but was bigger than any two of the others put together. The shaved head and chin scar identified the man as Champ Noon, the Black Crabs' leader and chief enforcer.

Calvin didn't know what he'd been a champion of. Since the Jamaican drug gangs began working the capitol, though, Noon had earned his nickname all over again. He was about the best in the business at killing people with his bare hands—the slower the better.

If Champ Noon was out here tonight, then Calvin Pitts and his Deacons had a fight on their hands, whether the big man they'd encountered the previous night showed up or not.

Pitts raced down the alley to the house so fast that he didn't check his back. He realized that only when Sam Goose let him in. Knowing that he could have gotten himself killed made him cold for a moment.

He'd have felt even colder if he could have seen the two hard eyes focused on his house from two hundred feet down the alley. The eyes scanned the area, recording every feature of the house and its yard.

Then the Executioner signaled Sergeant Chuyen to hold his position and began his final approach.

5

Bolan made his final approach as silently as a cat stalking prey. Long-range fire seldom hit its target, but it always alerted even the sleepiest sentries. It could also hit innocents, if there were any in the area. Making a move on this short notice and limited intelligence, Bolan couldn't be sure. So he followed his ironclad rule for approaching targets such as this: pack all the firepower in the world, but give the other side the first shot.

So far it had worked. Bolan was alive and his conscience, if not his body, was free of scars.

The garage was even more battered than the house itself. The walls showed as much bare wood as peeling paint, and the roof had more holes than tar paper. Bolan cautiously pulled the handle of the garage door. It came off in his hand, and the door let out an agonizing creak.

No cover that way. The warrior crouched by the rusty back gate and studied the rear of the house again. Still no lights, but there was movement in one of the second-floor windows and behind the screen of the back door. The gang sentries hadn't succeeded in keeping a good lookout without exposing themselves.

That didn't help Bolan, because he couldn't be sure those moving shadows were a drug lord's hardmen. His immediate problem was to get close enough for confirmation.

The backyard was more shadow than light, but anyone crossing the open grass would still show up too well and too soon. To the left, running from the garage to the house, was a tangle of weeds and sagging trellises that must have once been a garden.

Bolan slipped behind the garage and gripped the edge of the roof above the door. It creaked but not loudly, and held as he swung himself up onto the roof. There he was in shadow. He lay spread-eagled until he was sure no one in the house was aware of his presence.

His chin just above the tar paper, the Executioner crawled across the roof. He felt the rotten roof beams sag under his weight. With relief the warrior dropped to the ground on the house side of the garage.

From that point on a standard low crawl kept him out of sight nearly all the way to the house. Just as he was slipping around the largest trellis somebody opened the back door, pistol up and probing.

The chances of finding innocents in the house shrank again. They weren't gone, though. Bolan crossed the last forty feet to the back door in a rush.

The gunman inside heard him but didn't retreat. Instead he stepped forward, just far enough to be clearly visible. Bolan plucked the man out the door and flung him down on the lawn.

The gunner had no chance to shoot. He tried to shout, but having his face shoved hard into unmowed, trash-littered grass stifled the noise. Thunder rolled in the north, drowning out the scuffle.

"Who's in there?" Bolan growled.

"I can't—"

"You're dead, friend," the warrior said in a graveyard voice. "Only question is, dead slow or dead fast?"

"The Deacons," the man gasped. He tried to roll over, but Bolan held him pinned. "You with the Black Crabs?"

"I'm asking the questions. Any civilians in there?"

"No. God, you're hurting—"

"You sure?"

"Just six Deacons, but listen, man. We got the Black Crabs comin' in from the other side. You run with us tonight, and Whaley'll give you your own—" The gang member reached for his backup piece.

The silenced Beretta coughed twice, the second shot lost in another thunder roll. The man spasmed, toes and fingers gouging the hard ground, then went limp.

A second gunner crossed the threshold. Bolan uncoiled and the Beretta spit more 9 mm death. The man lurched backward, mouth open in a silent shout of warning, then fell out of sight.

The Executioner plunged past the corpse into the house, to be met by a burst of autofire from an Uzi near the stairs. He dived to the left, nearly taking a door off its hinges with his shoulder, and landed rolling.

More bullets chopped up the floor, the wall and the door. Bolan could taste plaster dust on his lips. At the moment the man with the stuttergun was in command of the situation.

At least he thought he was. Bolan decided to change the man's mind with a grenade—CS gas, not thermite, because it was too soon to set the house on fire. Burning houses drew firemen, who had no business in a battle zone.

Bolan removed a CS grenade from his combat harness, then threw it from a prone position. The gas billowed up the stairway, along the hall and into the side room. The warrior held his breath until he heard the man climbing the stairs through the cloud of gas.

The hitter arrived at the top of the stairs as Bolan reached the hall. The Executioner directed a 3-round burst from the 93-R up the stairs. It bucked against the warrior's powerful hands, firing without the shoulder stock, but it was accurate enough.

Hardman and Uzi crashed back down the steps. Another gunner showed up, but ducked back before Bolan could get off a shot.

Then a half dozen automatic weapons went off in front of the house, drawing response from up the stairs. As a hail of bullets tore through the front wall of the structure, Bolan felt one sear his left calf, and a splinter gouge his right shoulder.

The hall had quickly become a death trap. Bolan dived back into the room he'd just vacated. It wasn't the best place to carry on the fight, but at least it was out of the line of fire.

With the CS gas still hanging in the air, Bolan had to shut the door. That reduced one risk, but added another. The room had only one other exit—a boarded-up window. The warrior shifted to a corner where he could command both the window and the door, and listened to the raging battle.

After the initial flurry, it was now down to an occasional shot, as somebody either eased his nerves or imagined that he had a target. Bolan would have bet that the other side was the Black Crabs, another Jamaican drug gang that happened to have business with Whaley's people the same night the Executioner came calling. Under other circumstances it would have been funny. The Executioner, survivor of a hundred deliberate attempts on his life, was in danger of being caught in the cross fire of a gang battle.

Except that death was never funny to the man who died, and Mack Bolan knew that many other deaths would follow his. The deaths of innocent people, victims of the predators who would no longer have fear standing between them and their prey.

So he'd laugh later, if then. Now he had to use this lull in the action to make his move. He was studying the closet wall, looking for weak spots, when he heard someone shouting from upstairs.

CALVIN PITTS KNEW that talking with any mess of Black Crabs led by Champ Noon was likely a waste of time. He wouldn't have even thought of it if he'd had something to lose. The worst that Noon could do was kill him, and right now he'd likely do it faster than the Deacon, if Pitts messed up again tonight. He'd already lost three of his people, which cut him back to four. Champ had at least six, seven if you counted him as two.

Pitts crawled to the main window of the front bedroom, kept his head just below the windowsill and shouted.

"Hey, Champ Noon. We gotta talk, not shoot."

"You on our turf, man. What's to talk about?"

"We got somebody big downstairs. He hurt us some, but I think maybe we hurt him more. You help us take him out, and we go home."

"You lyin', man."

"Lord Jesus, Champ man. There is *no* way I'm lyin' about the man. You know what he did last night. This one, he's the same for damned sure."

"Maybe we let him do a number on you. Maybe he shoot himself dry, before he gets all of you. Then we got *nobody* on our turf who don't belong here."

"Champ, you—" No. Not even in this kind of situation was Pitts going to call Champ Noon crazy in the head. The big man *was* crazy. Everybody knew that. They also knew about the people he'd killed very slowly for saying so. One of them was a woman.

"Champ, this man, I don't think he's fightin' just the Deacons. When he gets through with us, he come after you."

"What the hell, you sayin' you got Batman locked up downstairs?" Pitts's mouth suddenly felt less dry. Champ sounded almost like he was willing to listen.

"This man's from no comic book, let me tell you," Pitts said. "What do you say, Champ? You send in two men, I'll send down two. The rest of us stay put, just in case somebody else comes around to join the party. That way we got him pinned back and front."

"If this man ain't what you say he is, Calvin, I'm going to hurt you considerably."

"That's better than being dead, which is the only other way to go tonight."

A grunt was Champ's only answer. A moment later a Deacon lookout whispered that he was coming across the street.

"Packing?"

"Not that I can see, but the man behind him, that's a MAC-10 if I ever saw one."

Right now, an Ingram subgun didn't bother Pitts. If Champ helped him deal the big killer out of tonight's game, he could bring a goddamned tank as backup.

BOLAN DIDN'T CATCH every word of the shouted conversation. The closet walls muffled part of it, and the growing thunderstorm outside wiped out more. The warrior was also busy, gouging a peephole through a weak spot in the crumbling plaster and ancient lath.

His work and the conversation ended at about the same time. The Executioner had plenty of time to squat in position, eye to the peephole, the Desert Eagle in his hand. He also had a thermite grenade in place, rigged so that anyone opening the door would set it off right under his feet. Bolan had been a sniper, but the Special Forces cross trained their A-teams.

The front door opened. Feet grated on broken glass and plaster. A man almost too large to be real loomed on the threshold. Behind him stood a smaller figure, holding an Ingram subgun.

Bolan held the Desert Eagle far enough from the wall that loose plaster wouldn't block the muzzle. Then he slammed three .44 Magnum rounds through the wall, toward the big man.

Two of them hit. But even with two of the huge slugs in his body, the big man stayed on his feet. He swayed like a tree in a high wind, the only sound from his mouth a bubbling cough as he tried to shout or scream. Finally, like that same tree finally going over, he crashed to the floor.

The subgunner shouted angrily and waved to the hardman behind him. Then he leaped over his leader's body and out of Bolan's line of vision.

He reappeared seconds later, flaming like a torch as thermite ignited his clothes, screaming as the flames consumed him. Bolan put the man out of his agony with a mercy round, then dropped all his weapons and threw his shoulder at the wall.

Laths cracked, plaster crumbled and a man-sized gap opened up in the ancient wall. Splinters punctured parts of the blacksuit and patches of skin under it, but the Executioner had a clear shot at the men coming at him. It didn't hurt that as they bunched up in the doorway, there were enough of them to make an unmissable target.

Bolan took out two of them with the 93-R, then reloaded the .44 and retrieved the Weatherby rifle. The survivors had run back down the front walk. If they didn't have the sense to keep on running, some long-range shooting would finish them off.

Cautious of his back, the Executioner crawled to the front window. As he sat up to aim the Weatherby, a burst of gunfire tore into the wall above his head. He whirled around to see a figure behind the rising flames in the hall, darting for the back door.

The man had missed an easy kill, but if he kept his head he'd live to fight another day. Bolan couldn't take the time to pursue his adversary.

Then everybody except the Executioner seemed to be shooting at once. The men upstairs and the men across the street were hurling lead at one another. The man in back was shooting too, but not toward Bolan. Somebody out in the alley was firing an M-16.

Almost as soon as it started, the gunfire from the hardman behind the Executioner ended in a grisly scream. Bolan knew who'd been using the M-16. Chuyen had joined in, orders or no orders, unable to resist an easy and legal target.

Bolan returned to the window, the Weatherby ready. Eye locked to the scope, he scanned the vacant lot. One man was lying still, another writhing. The third was trying to hide behind the first man and a rusted-out oil barrel.

In the next moment the man learned just how badly he was hidden. The Executioner drilled a round into the guy's head, which blew the man backward halfway to the lot wall.

By now the fire was spreading so fast that Bolan was coughing from the smoke. The flames also blocked his path to the stairs. If the Deacons were still upstairs, they were going to have to take their chances with the fire instead of with the Executioner. Even if they survived, the house and everything in it were shortly going to be ashes.

The side window of the living room was also boarded up, but the boards were loose. Bolan pried two free, and climbed out.

He landed in a pile of garbage, then had to burrow in the filth, as bullets whipped overhead.

"Chieu hoi!" he shouted, which was the agreed code of recognition he'd established with Chuyen.

The shooting stopped. *"Chieu hoi!"* came the response. Bolan sprung to his feet, collected his weapons and headed for the back alley. With sirens in the distance it was time to leave.

CALVIN PITTS and his three surviving men slid off the roof of the front porch half a minute after the last of the Black Crabs went down. If the Deacons cut hard right, they might just get out alive.

It might have landed them right back in trouble, too, because sirens were coming from that direction. The fire department came first, however. Three big yellow trucks swung around the corner, the firemen hanging on like monkeys. The howl of the sirens drowned out the thunder, and new arrivals didn't have attention to spare for a quartet of grimy Jamaicans jogging east.

By the time the police arrived Pitts had led his men one way, and Bolan and Chuyen had returned to their Pontiac by another. Then the thunderstorm finally kept its promise of rain, and a roaring downpour joined the thunder and lightning.

The rain saved the firemen some work by making it impossible for the fire to spread to neighboring houses. They hadn't planned to do more than that anyway, as the house was already lost. The battalion chief was on the radio to the arson squad when the police arrived.

The police weren't as happy about the rain. For one thing they didn't have the firemen's slickers and helmets. For another there were a lot of bodies lying around, and every drop of rain washed away clues about how they got there.

Both parties couldn't search for remaining bodies or clues until the rain slacked off. By then, Pitts was on the telephone to Deacon Whaley. Bolan and Chuyen were safely out of the area.

Chuyen had gone home, so happy that he would have cut a notch in the butt of his rifle if Bolan hadn't reminded him that it was plastic.

"Save the notches until this fight is over and you can hang the rifle on your wall," he told Chuyen.

"You think we fight again?" the sergeant asked.

"I'm certain we will."

Chuyen grinned and left the warrior's motel room, no doubt to pass that bit of wisdom onto the White Tigers.

Bolan shrugged. The White Tigers were going to deal themselves into this game, regardless of what he and Hal Brognola said. The best anybody could hope for was to make them play by the same rules as the Executioner.

6

"That's just perfect," Deacon Whaley said into the telephone. "No, really. It couldn't be better. We won't have any connection with it, and the man will still be deader than Bob Marley. What? No, I don't like this man's music a whole lot either. The sooner he stops playing, the better for all of us. Thanks."

Whaley hung up the receiver and turned to Calvin Pitts. Pitts was sitting in front of his boss's desk, which was better than standing. It was better so far as it meant the Deacon wasn't absolutely down on you.

On the other hand it was harder to manage a quick draw from the big armchair, unless you had your piece in a shoulder holster. Pitts's holdout gun, a 2-shot .22, was in the waistband of his trousers. He could feel its finger-sized butt digging into his belly muscles as if it were red-hot.

"Know who that was?" Whaley asked conversationally.

"At a guess, King Harris. Was he drunk or sober?"

"How often is he sober?"

"Not often enough for his own good."

"You thinkin' what I might be thinkin'?"

The holdout gun now felt not only red-hot but ten times as heavy. There were two times when Deacon set this kind of test on you: when he was thinking of promoting you and when he was thinking of wasting you.

Pitts got his breathing under control. He decided that he'd rather be a corpse than a coward if he had the choice. But maybe that wasn't all Whaley was offering him.

"If you're thinking his people might need a new boss fairly soon, I might agree with you."

"Thinkin' that the boss could be named Calvin Pitts?"

"Not unless another boss named Deacon Whaley says so."

Whaley nodded, grinned and pulled out a rum bottle. "Calvin, I heard how you handled that fight last night. It could've been done better. I've also seen it done a hell of a lot worse. Once I did it worse myself, when I'd been around long enough to know better.

"'Sides, anybody who misses the Black Crabs got real funny tastes in friends. I owe you one for that."

Whaley poured rum. "Won't be taking over the Kingdom, though, not real soon. I've got a little deal going with King Harris. He brings in our big friend's head, I'm going to owe him too much to mess with his people for a while.

"So I'm gonna pay what I owe him by sending him some real good men. You and Sam Goose, for starters, and each of you pick a couple more. You and the King, you ought to be like this—" Whaley crossed his fingers "—in a month. You take his orders like you take mine, too, unless he decides to send you after me."

"What if he does?"

"Play it like it sounds. If he just goes on drinkin', though, won't be more than another month or two before his people are taking orders from you."

Pitts tossed down the rum. It made all kinds of sense, seeing that King Harris would probably be in the drunk ward in a few months. Then his people would be orphans fighting for turf *and* leadership. Anybody who came along and spared them that mess of grief would be thought kindly of.

They might even be grateful enough to guard Pitts's back from both Whaley and the big man.

MACK BOLAN LISTENED in silence as Hal Brognola described the crack house run by the Black Crabs. Occasionally he interrupted to ask a question, but Brognola's usual answer was "No information on that."

Bolan finally stopped interrupting. Brognola and the police had done a good job of putting together a picture of the crack house by interrogating the Black Crabs survivors. They did so by moving in on them while they were still shell-shocked and wondering what was going to hit them next.

"If you take this place down, Striker, there won't be enough Black Crabs left to make a decent gumbo," Brognola finished. "But there's a wild card."

"Anybody we know?"

"How about the Silent Brotherhood?"

"What are they doing down here, unless they've decided to take me out on general principle?"

"I never heard the Brotherhood had principles. Anyway, it's not you. The rumor runs that they're moving in on D.C. to help purify the nation's capital from the evils of drugs, nonwhites and anything else they don't like.''

Like any right-wing terrorist organization, the Silent Brotherhood had a long list of things they didn't like. Some of them were things Bolan didn't like, either, such as drugs. Journalists with terminal stupidity had sometimes decided this coincidence made Bolan a ''fascist.''

''How much is there to the rumor?''

''I checked with the FBI. They came up with zero.''

That could mean stonewalling. There wasn't much love lost between the FBI and the leadership of Stony Man Farm. The Silent Brotherhood was an exception, though. The FBI took them seriously and would accept help from anyone who offered.

''Could it be a rumor somebody's planted to make the locals nervous?'' Bolan asked. His instincts had told him the answer before he put the question into words. He was merely looking for confirmation, not to mention warning Brognola that he'd move on the Black Crabs anyway.

''That's my guess, too. Your next few targets will be in pretty rough turf, places where a white man tends to stand out, and where even the 'law-abiding' citizens are packing. Add a rumor that somebody with your description is blowing away innocent nonwhites for some right-wing goon squad...''

''Right. Law-abiding citizens won't just be packing. They'll be out patrolling and maybe a little trigger-happy.''

"Exactly," Brognola said. "It's possible that you could be shot by some neighborhood vigilante. Maybe this one time you should back off."

"Maybe not. If whoever spread this kind of rumor gets the results he's looking for, a lot of people could suffer."

"I had to say it, Striker."

"And I have to do it, but thanks for your concern. I'll take my chances."

"Well, why not even up the odds a little by waiting until the police slip a few undercover people into the area?"

"That could take too long, Hal, particularly if you don't have any hard data for them. And what if the Black Crabs have somebody inside the D.C. police?"

Brognola remained silent, and Bolan pressed his advantage. "If the Black Crabs get any warning, they'll clean up the operation. If I go in and don't find anything, it'll look bad. But if I go in and the place is wall-to-wall crack, the neighbors will know I'm on their side.

"They're the ones who are on the firing line, Hal. If somebody makes their kids and their streets safer, they won't care where he comes from—or if he's black, white or purple."

"Okay, Mack. You win. But come back in one piece, okay?"

"Deal."

KING HARRIS WAS SOBER tonight. He knew that his men were looking hard at his drinking. Some were doing more than that like talking to other gangs—the Deacons, in particular.

He didn't like that. But nobody gave a rat's ass for what he liked or didn't like if he couldn't produce. After tonight they'd know he could produce. And "they" would mean not just his own people, but Deacon Whaley, too.

The Deacon would have to back off from whatever plans he had for the Kingdom, particularly if Harris made the big man his personal kill, or at least was on the spot when the man went down.

More than back off, maybe. Even cut Harris in on a piece of whatever the Deacon had going down with the Vietnamese. That would be real fine, if it happened. Harris didn't much like the Vietnamese. The good ones tried to fight drugs and the bad ones tried to grab too big a piece of the drug action. The fewer Vietnamese, the better, Harris decided.

The van groaned as the driver shifted gears for a hill. Harris pulled a cheap vinyl duffel bag onto the seat beside him and removed an Uzi. He had never fired one, except on the range, but he had five 30-round magazines and Bonefingers, the armorer, had checked everything out.

That amount of ammo should be enough for even the biggest, baddest man who ever made the mistake of tangling with Jamaicans. And if it wasn't, King Harris had his old .45, with eight notches on its butt. The gun had saved his life three times. It fitted his hand as if it grew there, and *nobody* was going to get out alive when he drew down on them.

BOLAN DROVE into the area in another anonymous car, this one a dirty brown Chevy Nova. He wore the blacksuit and had packed the usual weapons for a quick hit-and-run. The Weatherby would be useless in an area more densely built-up than Anacostia.

The shoulder-stocked 93-R, the Desert Eagle, plenty of ammunition and some incendiary and demolition charges should be enough to do the job. If he did get into a shooting match, he could keep it up long enough to blow the house and keep the bad guys' heads down while he retreated.

He hoped the civilians in the area would keep out of it. One of the disadvantages of being a one-man operation was that you didn't have anybody for crowd control.

An argument for taking Sergeant Chuyen along? Maybe, but not a strong one. The sergeant was a little quick on the trigger. If he blew away some innocent, it would be on Bolan's conscience more than his.

Also, whoever was trying to mess up Jamaican-Vietnamese relations would already have a lot of his work done for him. Bolan always tried to avoid situations that the criminals could exploit.

The neighborhood looked like bad turf, but there were quite a few people on the street, many of them women and children. To reduce the danger of their getting caught in the cross fire, Bolan parked in an alley on the far side of a public-housing development.

He checked his map with a penlight. The development should cover one flank, and by going a little out of his way he could stay in the alleys all the way to the shack.

After that, one undisturbed minute should be enough.

AUGIE, THE BLACK CRAB on guard in the crack shack was thinking that tonight was too slow. So damned slow you'd think something was up. Like maybe somebody hitting the place.

Could be; he knew what'd been going down. But there was only the two of them—him and Willie—a little crack and a lot of cash.

They didn't have orders about staying. So if something bad did come down, they were going to take the money and run so fast that their shadows wouldn't catch up with them until they were back at the Black Crabs' safehouse. If that wasn't safe enough to keep the hit off their backs, they were going to keep running, right out of D.C. and all the way back to the island.

With what they had ready to go in Willie's trash bag, they could live real good back home until they were too old to care if living was good or not.

"Hey, Augie," Willie called from the back. "Got some action down the street. Van just pulled up."

"How many?"

"Can't see. It's got curtains and they down. But I seen it before. That's a Kingdom van. King's personal wheels."

"Shit." It would be just like King Harris to go after the Black Crabs, especially now that Champ Noon and some of his best people were dead. Harris was a damned shark, always sniffing around for a wounded fish.

Augie pulled the door shut, locked it and checked the ground-floor rooms. Nobody there sleeping off a dose, snorting up, or screwing. In fact nobody there at all.

As Willie went upstairs to bag the money, Augie went to the back door. He held his Llama .32 in one hand and pushed the door open with the heel of the other. He held his breath as his head cleared the door frame, looking both ways along the alley.

"Shit," he said again. This time it came out sounding almost like a prayer. The man coming up the alley from the development side was big and rangy. He moved like a predator and held an automatic in one big hand. He was masked and gloved, but between the glove and the sleeve of what looked like a black running suit the guard saw pale skin.

The dude was white. No doubt about it. Augie drew back inside the house, but as he did, he saw movement behind the white man.

Four, five more men, were walking along behind the first one. Black dudes, real quiet, some of them almost as big as the man they were following. He'd bet some of them were packing, too.

Just then, Willie started down the stairs. Augie softly closed the door, locked it, then hurried up to meet him. The man stared.

"What are—"

Augie quickly explained. Willie listened until he was almost done, then something seemed to dawn on him.

"Yeah. It fit that rumor, about the neo-Nazis. That must be their hitter. Looks like the neighborhood's ready for him, though."

"Fine. Let them keep each other busy."

Augie wanted to shake Willie, but the other man had his free hand on the butt of his automatic. "Willie, what if we stay and help? Rumor says this is one bad dude. The neighborhood boys may need us. If they do, and we help them, what happens when the Kingdoms hit?''

An even brighter light dawned in Willie's eyes. "Yeah. Take out the Kingdoms, and where does that leave us."

"Running for boss of the Black Crabs, instead of back to the island, that's where."

Willie nodded. "Wait down here or go back upstairs?"

"Upstairs. I hear this guy likes grenades."

THE EXECUTIONER KNEW that he was being followed. The men behind him weren't the most expert tails he'd ever faced. Yet he still felt a prickling sensation between his shoulder blades. He didn't enjoy having his back bare to so many armed men who probably thought he was an enemy.

Somewhere along the last fifty feet of the alley he'd have to turn to confront them. Evasion would be even quieter, but they would follow him. In such a populated area innocents could get hurt.

There were no other options—fight it out or talk it out there in the alley even if it gave the crack dealers a warning. Right now the men who thought the Executioner was an enemy were more dangerous than the men who knew he was.

The click of a safety snapping off didn't surprise Bolan. He started to turn, leathering the Beretta, and shifted to one side at the same time. If he had his back to a solid wall, they'd have to shoot rather than try to grapple him. More than likely they weren't professionals, and that meant there was a chance to talk them down.

The roar of a heavy automatic *did* surprise Bolan. It surprised the five men following him even more. They were trying to get out of the alley as the bullet struck the cracked asphalt. Sparks flew, and one of the men screamed as the bullet ricocheted into his body.

Bolan vaulted over a trash Dumpster, drawing the Beretta as he landed. It took him a second to reorient himself and to identify the crack house. Then he spotted the silhouette of a man with an automatic in a dormer window.

It wasn't the best target he'd ever had, but Bolan's three 9 mm rounds knocked the man back into the attic. Most of the window followed, except for what tinkled and crashed down into the alley.

It was too long a throw for a grenade, but he hadn't checked the house for innocents anyway. Bolan studied the alley and had just planned his approach when he heard feet scuffing on the pavement.

He whirled. The Beretta was up and aimed, but not before the man with a Colt Commander had his aimed at Bolan's chest.

"Freeze, you Nazi mother," the man growled.

7

The pistol shots made King Harris jump. He was high, but he was still nervous. This was the first time he'd been so far out in front in years.

It felt good, though, even if it scared him a bit. He'd do it again if he could, and that would be another one up on Deacon Whaley. The Deacon hadn't been out in front with a gun in his hand in five years.

"Maybe somebody else's hitting them tonight," one of Harris's companions suggested.

"Maybe," Harris said. "No sweat for us if they have to look both ways."

It *would* be sweat, and maybe blood, too, if the Kingdoms accidentally blew away somebody from a gang who just wanted a piece of the Black Crabs' turf. But if the Kingdoms were careful, they wouldn't do anything that couldn't be settled with a piece of the Crabs' turf.

"All right," he said. "Two in the front, one to cover the back. Driver's coming down the alley when he sees the fire, or in ten minutes." He tapped his gold watch.

Two heads jerked in nods. A second Uzi and an Ingram came into view, and unsnapped holster flaps showed the butts of automatics. The man with the Ingram nodded again and darted toward the darkest path to the alley. King Harris waited until he disappeared, then hoisted his own Uzi and stepped out.

BOLAN DIDN'T MOVE. The man with the Colt took this as obeying the order to freeze until he spotted the Beretta still in Bolan's hand.

"Drop it!"

Bolan frowned. "We need to talk."

"Not with that in your hand. Drop it, or I count three."

Reluctantly Bolan put down the Beretta. The man hadn't noticed the big .44, and Bolan still had his unarmed-combat skills as well. The two together still might not be enough against a man who looked as though he wanted to shoot first and listen afterward. And he had the drop on the Executioner.

It was a fairly select company of people who'd gotten the drop on Mack Bolan this easily. Most of them were no longer around to boast about it. Those few who were, mostly were like this man—an innocent, guilty of nothing worse than mistaken identity.

Bolan decided to rely on a quick tongue. "I'm here for the same reason you are."

Whatever the man had expected from his captive, it wasn't that. He looked blank, then somebody behind him asked, "What reason's that?"

With two people on hand, Bolan had to be even more careful. If these men had any connection with the Black Crabs, he was *not* in a good situation. He had to gamble on both men being on the trail of neo-Nazis.

"Clean out the Black Crabs' operation," Bolan replied.

He heard a safety snap off. The direction hinted that a third man was within shooting distance. It wasn't an encouraging sound.

"Who do you run with?"

"Nobody. I'm free-lance. Name's Rance Pollock."

"Yeah," somebody said. "Free-lance killer for hire. Who's payin'?"

"The Black Crabs will, if you let me get to them," Bolan said. He tried to keep his voice quiet and patient. If the Black Crabs had enough men in the house to counterattack, they might catch him and the neighborhood protective association arguing. Bolan expected that he could survive. He wasn't sure about the local talent.

"They really have somethin' in there, the Black Crabs?" the man with the Colt said.

"I don't know why you think I'd be wandering around here tonight if they didn't," Bolan replied.

"Shh," came another voice. Then added, "Rackie, you know the Black Crabs are pushin' their shit in that house. This man wants to clean it out, and you want to stand here all night with a gun up his ass while they call for help?"

The voice was deep and commanding, but unmistakably a woman's. Bolan saw the man with the Colt flinch.

"Mama Ruth, I told you to stay clear."

"Well, it's a good thing I didn't—"

"Excuse me, ma'am." Bolan cut her short as calmly as he could. "But we're in pistol range of the house." He heard the woman suck in her breath. "They've al-

ready hit one of your people. I'm a professional. So
are the ones inside. Your men probably don't have
quite as much experience.''

"We got enough that we don't need to sit on our
asses out here while you blow the Black Crabs away,"
Rackie said indignantly.

Bolan wanted Rackie to button his lip. The local
men were determined to have somebody with the Executioner when he moved in—whether that somebody could handle himself in a firefight or not.

This mission was turning into a great one for un-
wanted passengers. Bolan didn't have to like it, but the
neighborhood men had a point. They had to have a
witness for what he did and found inside the house.
Otherwise they couldn't be sure he wasn't from the
Silent Brotherhood.

"Okay, ah, Rackie—"

"That's Rackham," the man said sharply.

"Okay, Rackham. Follow me to the door. You stay
there as security while I scout. When I say it's clear,
you come on up. If you hear shooting, take cover
where you can watch the door. They might get past
me, trying to escape."

"Uh-huh. I'm with you all the way. You don't draw
down on nobody tonight, if I'm not there to see it."

Bolan took a deep calming breath. "All right. Then
pick a second man to play security. We need somebody at our backs, or they can shoot us through the
head without hitting any brains."

The woman laughed at that. "All right," she said.
"Louis, you work okay with Rackie. You take rear-
guard. Okay, Mr. Pollock?"

"If Louis knows his job—"

"I've worked security. That enough?"

Hardly, Bolan thought, but it would have to do. They'd spent more than enough time arguing. Bolan had eliminated the risk of being shot on the spot by the neighborhood's self-appointed counterterrorist squad. Now all he faced was the risk of being shot by the Black Crabs *and* having innocent dead on his conscience.

As Bolan moved out of the shadows, he saw another man do the same a hundred feet down the alley. It was hard to tell in the darkness, but the man looked as if he were carrying an Uzi.

The man had no attention to spare for anything except the rear of the house that belonged to the Black Crabs, and he made sure nobody could see him. To Bolan and his companions, the man might as well have been wearing a neon sign.

"Who's—" Rackie began before Louis silenced him with a shoulder grip.

Bolan didn't know, either, but luck saved him from having to admit it. The man took a position out of sight, twenty-five feet away from the rear of the house. He pulled a grenade out of his pocket and pulled the pin.

The Executioner drew his Desert Eagle and sighted on the man. If the grenade went anywhere near Bolan and his improvised team, the mystery man was going to be dead before it blew.

Instead the man darted out into the alley and raised his arm behind his head. The grenade flew high into the back window of the second floor. Seconds later eye-searing flame and the dense smoke of white phosphorus poured out of the house.

As it did, Bolan heard the front door crash in, and an Ingram and another Uzi open fire. Far down the alley he glimpsed a dark van, running with only its fog lights on. Obviously the newcomers weren't Black Crabs reinforcements.

Bolan slapped both men on the shoulder.

"Come on!"

"Could be the police," Rackham remarked.

"No way they'd use white phosphorus," Louis said confidently. "Rackie, you gettin' scared or somethin'?"

Rackie jumped up. The grenade thrower saw him and swung the Uzi, but Bolan swung the .44 faster.

The subgun's burst raked the sky and the back of the house. A pair of .44 Magnum slugs ripped the gunner from chest to throat and flung him down like a rag doll.

This time when Bolan said, "Come on," the two men followed without arguing.

AUGIE SHOUTED to Willie to get back, but it was too late. The WP grenade came in the window and exploded before he was out of the way. He'd been too eager to see what happened to the man he hit and eager to try to finish him off.

Willie was lucky in one way. He tripped, trying to avoid the grenade. As he went down his head hit the headboard of the bed. It was solid oak and knocked him out.

He never felt the phosphorus eating into him.

Augie didn't feel much, either, except for the sinking feeling that tonight he was going to go a lot farther than Jamaica. He didn't forget the satchel with the cash, which he grabbed in one hand, or the .32 Llama, which he held in the other.

He ran downstairs just as King Harris and his companion finished shooting up the door. They must have assumed that anybody in a position to shoot back had developed terminal lead poisoning. They charged through the bullet-riddled door into the hall without throwing another grenade.

That made the next few seconds a fairly even fight. Everybody had their guns out, and everybody fired at once. The Llama put a .32 soft-nose into King Harris's shoulder and gouged his side with a second.

The Ingram and the Uzi replied with a decisive amount of lead, even if Harris's shooting was a bit on the wild side. The subguns put half their bullets into the walls and ceiling, the other half into Augie.

He dropped the Llama and the satchel, his knees sagged—one of them had been shattered by a tumbler—and he came down the stairs in a perfect somersault. Hitting the floor broke his neck on top of his already fatal bullet wounds.

Unlike his victim, King Harris had plenty of time to start hurting. In fact he was hurting so bad that he screamed when he bent over to pick up the satchel.

"Let me grab that, boss," Jackson, his companion, said. The man scooped up the satchel and slung it over one arm. Then he gripped his Ingram one-handed and tucked the other arm around his boss's shoulders.

"Easy, man! Easy! I'm hurtin'."

"We get what's in this, it buys a lot of doctors. The kind that keeps their mouths shut. And we'll have it, not the Black Crabs."

Harris didn't answer. It hurt him too much just to move and breathe to have anything left over for talking. Jackson urged him to keep going.

They both heard an engine outside in the alley, then the screech of tires and somebody shouting in pain.

THE VAN ROARED up the alley as if trying out for the Indianapolis 500. The Executioner's two companions stayed safely under cover.

Another local man wasn't so smart. Suddenly struck by lightning or maybe by memories of too many Rambo movies, the man leaped out into the alley. He held a pistol in a two-handed grip as he stood directly in the van's path.

He got off three .38 Specials before the van driver hit the brakes.

Two more bullets went wild, as the van screeched, swerved and swung around almost a hundred and eighty degrees. By a miracle it didn't blow a tire or go over, even though it was on two wheels part of the time. The rear bumper caught the Rambo imitator and sent him flying across the alley.

The van's windshield was a webbed and crumbling mess. So was the back window. Unable to see the driver, Bolan warned his two companions to be alert. Then he caught the ladder on the back of the van and scrambled up to the roof.

From there Bolan could look into the blazing second-floor back room. The man he saw had to be dead.

As the warrior looked away, bullets punched up through the van roof, one just missing his right foot. At the same time he heard the back door of the house crash open, then footsteps and groans.

The Executioner rolled off the van roof toward the side of the house, landing in combat stance with the stocked Beretta ready. He had one bit of luck: the unwounded hardman was closer to him than King Harris and took the first half-dozen 9 mm rounds. The rest was shooting better and faster than his opponents.

Ten seconds later both Harris and his companion were on the ground in spreading pools of their own blood.

Bolan allowed himself a moment of satisfaction. The Kingdom was going to start to change hands in a bloody war of succession. The more drug pushers who killed one another in that war, the better off the city would be.

At that moment the Executioner became aware of a struggle on the other side of the van. He ran around the front, Beretta up and ready, to find Louis and Rackham with the driver down on the pavement. They'd disarmed him and were now taking turns pounding his head against a rough-looking piece of concrete. His scalp was already bleeding.

"Hold it!" Bolan demanded.

"Sure, I'll hold him and you take a turn with him," Rackham said. "Man, we were sure wrong about you. You know who this guy runs with?"

"King Harris."

Both men gaped, and one of them made a Jamaican sign against evil spirits.

"Sorry. I'm not a mind reader. Harris and one of his pet guns came out the back door when I was on the other side of the van. That was the shooting you heard."

"Then all we do is—"

"Tie this man up and take him with us," Bolan said. His tone would have stopped a charging rhinoceros. "We need information about who's left in Harris's gang. Otherwise we won't know how to finish them off."

As the two men started to look for rope, Bolan approached the man who'd been hit by the van. He was swearing too loudly for anyone seriously hurt, and the woman called Mama Ruth was already bending over him.

In the dim light Bolan could see that she was grayhaired, nearly six feet tall, and must have been a real beauty when she was younger. She was also pushing the man around like a rag doll as she probed for injuries.

"Busted collarbone, busted arm, maybe some cracked ribs," she said, as Bolan joined her. "We can take care of him."

Bolan opened his fieldkit. "How's the man who got hit with the first shots?"

"Tom's hurt himself worse droppin' a hammer on his foot. Just nicked his leg."

"Good." Bolan handed her a field dressing. "Slap this on him and carry him to the van."

"That thing ain't never goin' to run—"

"We don't know until we try it. I'm not going to carry these two guys to the nearest hospital."

Bolan saw her eyes narrow at the mention of "hospital." He then understood that she and her friends might not have any money or insurance, not to mention fear of the police and surviving drug dealers.

He left the woman and went back around the van, returning a few seconds later with the satchel. The woman's eyes widened as he opened it and she saw the bundled currency.

"I think you've got the best claim to it. That should take care of the bills. I have a few friends I can call to make sure the police don't hassle you. Now, what about that hospital?"

The woman's eyes narrowed as she studied Bolan. Then she nodded slowly.

By the time the casualties were bandaged, one of the men had managed to get the van moving. It sounded as if it were on its last legs, and he had to poke out the windshield and use the outside rearview mirrors, but it would run.

Bolan rode in the back of the van to within a block of the nearest hospital. Then at a red light he popped the rear door and leaped out.

"Hey!" the woman called.

"Remember, I have to make those phone calls."

"Well, sir, you surely haven't heard the last of Mama Ruth!"

8

"I have a nasty feeling that Mama Ruth is right." Bolan kicked off his shoes and lay down on the second bed in the room.

"About hearing from her again?" Hal Brognola asked.

"Right."

"Why is that a nasty feeling?"

"Maybe 'uneasy' would be a better word," Bolan amended. "I have enough on my plate keeping the Viets out of the line of fire. If I have to keep Mama Ruth and her Jamaican helpers from rushing into firefights, I might be too busy to deal with the bad guys."

"You could always accept Mama Ruth's help," Brognola pointed out.

Bolan looked sourly at his friend, as if not willing to dignify the remark with a response.

Brognola poured himself a cup of coffee, although he neither needed nor wanted it. It gave him something to do while he decided if the warrior deserved an apology.

"You were certainly right about one thing," Brognola said finally.

"What's that?"

"The Black Crabs. The police hauled in about a dozen more of them before sunrise."

"They won't be off the streets very long. Remember due process?"

Brognola not only remembered due process, he had practiced it for most of his career. He knew perfectly well that it had its place in the war against the predators. There had to be rules. But it helped if there was someone to operate outside the rules, when the predators exploited them and endangered innocent lives.

Brognola sipped at his coffee. There'd been more in Bolan's tone than a statement of fact.

"You sound like that's good news."

"I've heard worse." Bolan sat up, flexing from the waist. Superbly conditioned muscles rippled under a black T-shirt.

"If the Black Crabs all end up behind bars, Deacon Whaley gets their turf without having to fight for it. If the Black Crabs' hardmen come out just as Whaley's moving in, he'll have a fight on his hands."

"*Another* fight, you mean," Brognola said. "The street talk is that he's already moving in on the Kingdom."

"You're right. He won't get that without a fight, either. In a gang war like that, even bosses as high as Whaley have been known to get shot. If somebody keeps tempers hot by sniping the odd hardman, Whaley might wind up sleeping in his own safe."

"If he sleeps at all," Brognola said. To someone who didn't know Bolan, the line of reasoning might have sounded cynical. To Brognola it was simply the Executioner's ruthless realism.

He wasn't so sure about the outcome of the drug gangs' wars for turf. Innocent bystanders might get shot simply because some hardman didn't look before he opened fire. It was also possible that Deacon Whaley could win both of his fights. Then he could call D.C.'s drug scene his own.

As if he'd been reading Brognola's mind, Bolan shrugged. "Of course, Whaley might win. But if he does, he'll have a lot of new people and turf to digest. He might make enemies. Enemies who can talk, or even shoot. The bigger and fatter he gets, the slower he moves, and a slow-moving target is always easier."

Brognola recognized a trained sniper's professional judgment there, not just a play on words.

"At least he'll be an easier target if I don't have to worry about passengers," Bolan said. "I'll think of something to do about the Jamaicans, even if I have to call Mama Ruth myself. How are you coming on the White Tiger Society?"

Brognola had been expecting that question. He wasn't looking forward to what Bolan would say about his answer.

"Well, we have an ID on that Vietnamese who leaned on you. Ever heard of Colonel Ngo Phung?"

"I thought he was dead." One of the ARVN's most effective combat leaders as well as an intelligence expert, the colonel was supposed to have died during the fall of Saigon.

"Think again. And don't think too loudly about it outside this room. Officially he's still dead. In fact I'm damned sure he's working with the Company."

"Liaison to the White Tigers?"

"Yes, and at a higher level than you've ever been allowed to see. They probably aren't the only group he works with, either."

"I see. Which gives him a lot of influence over Viets the intelligence bureaucracy needs for work in Southeast Asia."

"Got it. If it gets out that Phung is alive and that *we* blew him helping you..." Brognola hesitated. "Well, nobody but the President could keep the Company from putting out a termination order on you after that."

"I'll take my chances, Hal. Do I send Phung around to you, or try to argue with him myself? I did cut him back to one man the first time."

"You might not be so lucky this time. We think Phung's tasted blood. He might try to put the squeeze on us to let his White Tigers off their chains."

Bolan lay back on the bed and stared at the ceiling. "Hal, does Stony Man have any assets Phung could use? And that would be safe to give him?"

Brognola understood the limitation. A good deal of Stony Man Farm's data was obtained from the intelligence establishment on condition that it went no farther than Able Team, Phoenix Force, or the Executioner. Handing NSA, DIA or CIA secrets to Colonel Phung to sweeten him might raise more than eyebrows.

"I'll check. Thinking of negotiating some limitations on the White Tigers' participation?"

"Why not?" Bolan asked. "If the colonel calls up, I think it's time to teach him a useful lesson."

"Which is?"

"A squeeze can go both ways."

"YOU WANT ME TO MOVE IN on the Black Crabs or don't you?" Deacon Whaley asked.

"They're not so many as you'd want, not now," Calvin Pitts said. He wasn't sure what his boss had in mind and decided to be cautious until he did.

"They'll be more when my lawyers pay a little call on the police. There's no 'probable cause' for holdin' half the ones they dragged in."

Lawyers who could go head-to-head with the D.C. prosecutors and police on drug charges didn't come cheap. Springing the Black Crabs was going to take a big bite out of the ChiCom million—if Whaley had it.

Pitts knew better than to mention money. Instead he shrugged. "I have to keep the ones outside together until your lawyers finish up. That's a tall job, just for me."

"Who said it was goin' to be you all alone?" Whaley said. His glare wasn't entirely a joke.

"Well, it seemed to me—"

"Seemin' and bein' are two different things, Calvin, my friend. Take my word for that."

"Yes, boss."

"You can also take a few people with you. Sam Goose, and anybody else you and he can work with. Four, five maybe. That better?"

It was a whole lot better, but Pitts didn't let on. He still wanted to know why Deacon Whaley was going to stick himself right into the war for the Black Crabs and Kingdom turfs. Sure, it meant grabbing the turf. It might also mean finding the big man in their way again, and a lot more of the Deacons dead.

One of them might be Pitts. Even if he wasn't, he could end up number two in a gang that had lost more than it could afford. If that happened, they'd be fighting just to defend their own turf.

"What's the matter, Calvin? You thinkin' I should wait for the ChiComs to tell me to wipe my ass?"

"Hell, no."

"Good. If I thought you were a crazy or a Red, we might have problems, you'n me." Deacon was still going after the lion's share of the D.C. drug scene, and as far as he was concerned the big man didn't count.

Whaley finally noticed that Pitts's attention was wandering. "What's really got into you, brother? You don't think the ChiComs could have bought us with a lousy million and a couple missiles?"

"No way. But there's another favor they might do, real cheap."

"Take out that man fightin' for the Viets?"

Pitts managed to put his glass down instead of dropping it. "Think they would?"

"We'd owe them one if they did. I want them owing *us*. I want them where if they want us to sneeze they got to ask nice and pay cash. Besides, what makes you think the man's workin' with the Viets?"

It was true. One incident didn't meant that the man and the Vietnamese were actually partners against the Jamaicans. It had convinced Pitts, but it might not convince the Chinese.

"Well, if he isn't, I'd like to know who he does run with."

"Me, too, brother. We can always ask, *after* we catch him. Meanwhile, you just think on running the Black Crabs. For me, remember. You start settin' up on your own, you and me gonna have to have a long talk."

BOLAN WAS ON HIS WAY to the Blue Mountain House an hour after the call from Mama Ruth. He'd have been on his way faster if he hadn't needed to arm himself and call Hal Brognola.

"I hope you can avoid a fight," was all Brognola said. "That might get the neo-Nazi rumors flying again."

"I don't think Mama Ruth's got a setup in mind."

"Probably not. But what if she wants something you can't give her? From your description, she isn't a person we want mad at us."

"Hal, you're really getting good at understatements in your old age," Bolan said, and hung up. With both the Desert Eagle and the Beretta safely leathered, he moved out as fast as the rush-hour gridlock let him.

That was so slowly, that by the time the traffic began thinning out Bolan was ready to park his car and walk the rest of the way. He got to the Blue Mountain House just as the dinner crowd was leaving.

His concern about standing out in a half-empty restaurant quickly vanished. The Blue Mountain House was a maze of little rooms, some of them private enough to hold an orgy if that was your idea of fun. It was also the kind of restaurant where anybody from a king to a beggar would fit in. Bolan, an expert at being inconspicuous, stopped feeling the itch between his shoulder blades that came from turning his back on a possible trap.

Nevertheless, he stayed alert as he walked into the room Mama Ruth had reserved. He saw that one of the waitresses was standing by the table, chatting like an old friend, even if she was young enough to be Ruth's daughter.

"Evenin', Mr. Pollock," the older woman said. "You got any taste for crab soup?"

"I understand the place ran out of it last night," Bolan said, giving the agreed-on recognition code.

"We expect to have some more in tomorrow night," the waitress said. Bolan looked hard at her. She was a handsome young woman, with wide brown eyes and a spectacular figure. But she wasn't supposed to be giving the third part of the recognition code.

The itch returned. From long habit Bolan's eyes had measured the distance to any door in a room where he faced danger. If this was a trap, it was going to be more dangerous to Mama Ruth and the waitress than to him.

The waitress caught the movement of Bolan's eyes. She reached down the front of her dress and very slowly pulled out a D.C. police badge.

"Mr. Pollock, I think you're entitled to an explanation of why we dragged you here."

Bolan didn't sit down. "Probably."

Mama Ruth pushed a chair toward him. "Goin' to take a while."

There was a point when caution might cost you vital information. Bolan decided that he'd reached that point. He took the chair and sat, shifting it so that he faced the door. He noticed that Ruth and the policewoman were just as careful about their backs.

The explanation was simple enough. Mama Ruth knew a lot of people in the Jamaican community who knew things that would break drug gangs. These people wouldn't talk to anybody who had to put their names down.

"The gangs come down pretty hard on anybody they think done too much talkin'," Ruth said. Like Hal Brognola, the older woman seemed to have a knack for understatement.

That brought in the policewoman, Sergeant Claire Brousson of the narcotics division as liaison. It also called for someone like Bolan, who could sanitize the information before he passed it on.

"What makes you think I can do that?" Bolan asked.

"The way you operated last night—" Claire began.

"Just hush, girl," Ruth said. "You didn't see him. I did. Seeing you, I figured you for either a crazy or somebody with connections where it counted."

"Well, if you're willing to gamble on my being the second—" Bolan began.

"We are," Claire said. Ruth raised her eyebrows and the policewoman flushed. "Sorry, Mama Ruth."

"Girl, you're in too much of a hurry. You can always go back into uniform. For us it's win this one or lose everything we came up here to find."

Bolan studied the two women. Mama Ruth looked as if she didn't know who he was, other than trustworthy. On the other hand Sergeant Brousson...

The policewoman was one of the many law-enforcement people who "officially" opposed the Executioner as a vigilante. "Unofficially," however, they'd fed Bolan vital information a dozen times and saved his life more than once. Sergeant Brousson looked like another helper. More cautious than most, because she was working through a civilian—one who would be in mortal danger if the drug lords knew about her.

She knew it, too. Bolan's rules about keeping innocents away from the fight were strict, especially when they didn't know what was going on or how to handle themselves.

On the other hand, when they were like Mama Ruth, already in the fight before the Executioner showed up, he could bend the rules. He'd had to, or too many animals with human shapes would still be prowling the world's streets.

"We can pass the information on in lots of different ways," Bolan said. "I'll go along with any way of getting it to me that doesn't make trouble for the witnesses. I won't be in any danger until I have the information and the gangs know it."

That was considerably less than the truth, and the looks both women gave him showed that they knew it.

"Don't know about you, but I think better on a full stomach," Mama Ruth said. "Girl, you want to go back to being a waitress long enough for us to get something inside us?"

9

Calvin Pitts decided that the ringing was really the bedside telephone, not his ears. He reached across the girl beside him and picked up the receiver.

"Hello?"

"Are you alone, brother?" It was Deacon Whaley.

"Not so's you'd notice."

"Get alone."

"Now?"

"Now."

Calvin prodded the girl in the ribs. She giggled as if it tickled. Then he slapped her on her bare buttocks. "Girl, you got until five to be out of this room."

"You serious, man?"

"One, two—"

At "three" the girl looked at Calvin's face and decided that he was serious. At "four" she decided he was serious enough for her not to waste time dressing. She grabbed her clothes and one shoe and darted for the door. It slammed shut behind her on "five."

Pitts locked the door again and found that he could walk almost normally on his way back to the bed. It still helped his head to lie down for his chat with Deacon.

"You alone *now*?"

"Yeah."

"You don't sound sure."

"Boss, what's comin' down? If it's heavy enough, and somebody's listenin', you know I'll get my ass blown away before you do."

"How about neither of us gets blown away, and you take out Mama Ruth?"

In spite of himself Pitts whistled. "How fast? She got a lot of friends from the island. They learn who did it, and some of them'll be lookin' up anybody who don't like us for help."

"They'll have to come after us personal, or go to the police. You think we can't handle that?" Deacon had obviously made up his mind. "I don't want Lady Big Mouth to see dawn tomorrow. If that means pulling men off the Black Crabs job—"

"No other way, boss. I'll need three, maybe four besides Sam Goose. Who she been talkin' to, by the way?"

"She's been talkin' to a whole bunch, and *they've* been talkin' to our big friend. Least I heard they're plannin' it that way."

If Mama Ruth and the big man were planning something against Whaley's interests, nothing short of killing both of them would stop it. Pitts knew Mama Ruth's reputation, and he'd seen the big man in action. "If our big friend's in on this, I could use thirty, maybe forty."

"I don't have them and you won't get them. But I'll have everybody who doesn't have a job keep an eye out for our friend. Anybody sees him, they tail, call in, and whichever one of us has people to spare sends them around. This guy's good, but even Superman had a weakness.''

THE OFFICE COMPLEX in Falls Church where the Stony Man people had their new message drop was itself new. It was one of the developments that sprouted as a result of the D.C. Metro's extension into the Virginia suburbs.

Only half the offices were rented, and nobody seemed to be working late in any of them as far as the Executioner could tell. He let himself in through the service entrance, flattened himself into an alcove as two cleaning women pushed a cart past, then started up the stairs.

He broke his climb several times, because his instincts told him that somebody had tailed him from the parking lot. Instincts, and seeing the same nondescript dark man in a green shirt and jeans three times since he left the lot.

The office complex had valet parking, but Bolan didn't want any of the staff to see him. Parking blocks away, then walking, was a reliable way of drawing any tail into the open. It also kept the fight between you and him.

Bolan finally stepped into the open on the seventh floor. He passed two law offices, three vacancies and a Federal Express drop box to reach the Lindquist and Kelly office. The small public-relations firm was quite legitimate and even turned a profit without the subsidy it got from Stony Man funds. Both partners were also combat veterans, cooperative without being too curious.

The warrior let himself into the office, used the after-hours combination to open the safe and dropped in the recording of Mama Ruth's informants. It held enough to make trouble for every drug lord in the D.C. area and to put them out of business.

Even so, the victory wouldn't be decisive or permanent. Society kept producing new criminals as fast as it cleaned up the old ones. Like garbage, you couldn't let either one accumulate or it would overwhelm you.

"Hopeless," however, was a dirty word in Bolan's vocabulary. The only situation that held no hope was being dead.

The Executioner waited in the office for ten minutes, to see if his tail would catch up. He heard nothing other than the rattle of something already loose in the new ventilation system.

He waited another five minutes, then called in the drop to Stony Man and got ready to move out.

He'd just locked the door behind him when his peripheral vision told him of a change in the scenery. The Federal Express box was casting a wider shadow.

Bolan had the 93-R drawn in the same moment as the shadow moved. He was an easier target than the man behind the box, but a faster shot. His first 9 mm round punched into the sheet metal of the box and threw the man's aim off. The ambusher's own two rounds chipped paint and shattered a panel light on the ceiling.

He never fired a third. Bolan had a clear target now and punched a 3-round burst into the gunner's chest. He sprawled on the floor in a puddle of blood. His shirt quickly turned dark, but it was originally silvery-gray rather than green. The tail had a partner.

Maybe more than one. That thought struck Bolan as a blast of rounds from what sounded like an Ingram stuttergun sprayed over his head.

By the time the next burst came the warrior was a fast-moving target. He sprinted down the corridor toward the atrium end of the building. The atrium ran from the second floor up to the tenth, with its own elevator running in a glass shaft. A man in the right position had a view in all directions, and the Desert Eagle had the range to hit anything in that view.

The Executioner was in the right position before he heard the sound of the subgunner in hot pursuit. He crouched, the .44's muzzle aimed at the corridor, then felt a bullet whiz past his ear and another sear his ribs.

Bolan was rolling to a new position as the echoes of the shots died. He was also recalculating the situation. Two against one with his position known was less favorable than he'd hoped. If the man above took advantage of the atrium's good visibility...

The Executioner's shift threw off his assailant's aim. The next two shots went wide, puncturing a fire extinguisher. The subgunner chose that moment to step out of the corridor.

He and Bolan saw each other at the same moment. The quick draw contest ended as two rounds from the Desert Eagle slammed the subgunner halfway down the corridor. His head cracked on the floor, his Ingram clattering beside him and skidding out of sight.

The elevator rose up the shaft.

The warrior risked being an easy target, trying to both reach the shaft and stop or jam the car before the man above could use it for his escape. The hardman wasn't hit and Bolan couldn't stop the elevator, either. It sailed past him, only its metal door visible.

The Desert Eagle could punch through the door as if it were cardboard, but what if the gunman had taken a hostage? Bolan moved again, even faster now that his enemy was temporarily unable to shoot.

Bolan got a clear view of the elevator as it descended. The hardman was alone, and standing at an angle that made it almost impossible to hit him. The Executioner was lining up the .44 Magnum for a final effort when a security guard ran into sight.

If the bullet ricocheted, the guard would be in danger. Bolan flung himself toward the stairs and ran down them three at a time. As he passed the fourth floor he heard a quick exchange of shots, the guard's .38 against a weapon firing .357 Magnums.

The warrior left the stairs on the third floor, hoping to get into position above the hardman undetected. But the two men had shifted, and a second guard had joined the fray.

The second guard let fly at Bolan, hitting the railing. Brass rods rang like gongs, and glass shattered, a piece stabbing into the Executioner's calf.

Shooting at Bolan, the second guard made a stationary target for the hardman. This time he made no mistake. The guard dropped his gun as a .357 slug ripped his shoulder, then died with a muffled scream as a second tore his chest.

The first security guard was now where he could neither shoot accurately nor be shot at. Bolan wouldn't mind if he stayed put.

Unlike the dead guard, though, the hardman knew which side Bolan was on. He knew the odds were still against him, and took advantage of the live guard's being out of the fight. He broke from cover and sprinted for the door.

Fear of ricochets kept Bolan's weapons silent. He vaulted the railing, felt pain stab through creased torso and punctured calf, but landed safely.

He came up from a crouch and ran straight for the door. Not only did he have to gain ground on the fleeing hardman, he also had to be out of range before the security guard decided that he was a bad guy.

Bolan did better with the second goal than with the first. He was out the door before the guard could do more than shout "Hey, you! Stop!"

The hardman was in sight but out of safe shooting range.

The warrior leathered the Desert Eagle and settled down to closing the range. His minor wounds began to be a major bother, and sweat stung his eyes as he ran through the humid D.C. night. But his breath flowed smoothly and so did his leg muscles, driving him down the street on the trail of his quarry.

There were alternatives to chasing the man, Bolan admitted. He was risking being led into another trap. But the Executioner couldn't let a cold-blooded killer get away. The security guard couldn't have been the man's first victim. He wouldn't be his last, either. Not unless someone intervened to end the killer's career tonight.

Bolan upped his pace.

The warrior hoped he could bring the man down without killing him. He wanted to hear what the hardman would say. It probably wouldn't be the truth, but dead men never said anything at all.

Another two minutes, and Bolan saw that the man was running for the Metro station. It was late, but not too late for the trains to be running. It wasn't too late for the station platform to hold a scattering of innocents, either.

The man cut down an alley, fired a wild shot at Bolan without even slowing, then was out in the open again. Bolan saw him plunge down the entrance of the station and followed without hesitation.

The escalators were motionless, one of them blocked off for repairs. Bolan saw two repairmen levering up a tread, and beyond them the fleeing hardman. Not a good angle for a shot, and once again the ricochet danger was too great.

The hardman lacked the Executioner's principles. He shot wildly twice, hitting nothing, but alerting the repairmen, who flattened themselves on the escalator. Bolan leaped onto the smooth metal strip between the two escalators and slid down.

He reached the bottom in time to see the hardman vault the turnstile and sprint down the stairs toward the platform. Late-night travelers scattered as the gunner dashed toward the overpass that crossed to the opposite track.

They didn't scatter enough to give Bolan a clear shot. He followed anyway, as an inbound train rolled out of the tunnel into the station. The hardman vanished behind the overpass railing.

The warrior stopped. It would be worth a lot to have the man reveal his position with another wild shot, but not enough to risk someone's life. Bolan got as much protection as he could manage from a bench and waited.

The doors of the train on the other track hissed shut. Then the lights along the edge of the platform on Bolan's side began blinking, the signal that another train was coming.

The first train began to move. As it did, the gunner appeared, balanced on the railing. Bolan guessed the man's plan—jump to the roof of the train and ride it clear. There wasn't much time, but the warrior saw that he had a clear shot.

The Desert Eagle sent echoes around the station, louder than the two trains. The man whirled, clutching at his shattered leg, and tried to raise his own pistol. Bolan was ready to shoot again if the man opened fire, but hoped he would fall back onto the overpass.

Instead he overbalanced and toppled over the railing, down onto the near track, just as the train rolled into the station.

Brakes hissed and bystanders shouted in horror. The hardman's scream was drowned out, as the wheels mangled him into something barely recognizable as a human being.

Bolan was looking down at what was left of the hardman when he saw two Metro police approaching. Both had their guns out, so he was careful not to make any sudden moves as he turned toward them.

"Ah, could we have that gun and maybe some ID?" the taller of the two officers said. He sounded like a man resigned to trouble no matter who Bolan was, but ready to do his duty regardless.

"I've got a better suggestion. I'll give you the gun, then I'll make a phone call and let you talk to my legal counsel."

When you got right down to it it wasn't a bad description of Hal Brognola. The Justice Department was certainly legal enough and would also be happy to counsel these well-intentioned policemen about arresting the Executioner.

10

Getting the Executioner out of the hands of the police was an interesting exercise for Hal Brognola. He had to persuade them to let Bolan go without revealing either Bolan's identity or his.

It helped that several people witnessed the dead gunner shoot up the station *before* Bolan opened fire. The police didn't know for certain that Bolan was one of the good guys, but they were willing to be persuaded.

It didn't help that Brognola had to conduct the whole argument over a less than secure line. It was also between midnight and 1:00 a.m.

The big Fed finally convinced them that Bolan was doing classified work that entitled him to go armed and that he'd been trying to make a citizen's arrest on the gunman. He would either testify at the coroner's inquest or at least submit a written deposition. And he would certainly post Bolan's bond not to leave the United States until the inquest.

"I assume that you made a reasonable effort to evade before you settled down to a shootout?" Brognola asked Bolan dryly when he got him on the line.

"Yeah. Remember the old rule that it takes one to start a fight, but two to break it off. I think you'd better have someone over to Lindquist and Kelly ten minutes ago. You might even want to consider moving them.''

Brognola gave a noncommittal grunt. Stony Man Farm's operations were as "black" as anything in the intelligence community, with a generous and completely untraceable budget. Still, it took time, money and labor to move a drop.

He was about to ask why Bolan hadn't turned on his tail before leading him to the drop, then realized that that would be second-guessing. Brognola had no energy left for the kind of argument that could lead to.

"We'll not only consider it, we'll do it. But you might want to move against Deacon Whaley before he hears about this shootout.''

"That's a negative, Hal. The first thing I do is drop by Mama Ruth's and get her to someplace safe. Then I can take out Deacon at leisure.''

"Someplace safe," Brognola said. "One of ours, of course.''

"Of course.''

"Don't tie yourself up getting her out of the picture.''

"Hal, Whaley's not going anywhere. Or if he is, it's likely out of business.''

Brognola was silent, thinking of a recent conversation with Colonel Phung and a slightly less-recent conversation with somebody too high up in the CIA for Brognola's peace of mind. The next moment, he wished he hadn't even thought about those conversations.

"Are the Viets popping up again?" Bolan asked.

"Not yet. But they will be, if you don't clean out Whaley before they get their act together."

"If they pop up too soon, Hal, they may get popped themselves."

"The CIA would take a very dim view of anything happening to Colonel Phung or his crew in the White Tiger Society."

"I hope they also know that Whaley still packs a lot of firepower. I'd like to cut it back some more before the Viets take the field."

"Forty-eight hours?"

"If you can grab Phung by the ankles for that long, it would help."

"I'll see what I can do. I'm not promising miracles or even results, just trying."

"Good enough for me."

Bolan seemed about to hang up, then added, "Hal, I'm going to change cars. See if you can stake out my old one. Somebody might get curious enough to wander by, and if we can grab him..."

"Will do."

SAM GOOSE DIDN'T HAVE any backup for his eyeballing of Mama Ruth's building. He didn't figure that he needed it, either, not at one o'clock in the morning. With two pieces—one of them silenced—any arguments would be short and not at all sweet for the other man.

The stakeout took twenty minutes from one side. Then a two-minute hike took him through an alley for the rest of the job. He could have walked around the block, since Calvin and the others were still on the way. But he didn't like getting that far from the target.

It was something he couldn't name, but when he stayed close to his target he could sometimes feel when they got a warning. That feeling had saved his life twice, and another time it saved two other men, as well. One of them was Calvin, which was one reason Sam Goose had a good place with Calvin in Deacon Whaley's army.

He'd have a better place after tonight, he was sure. Too many people had been scared of Mama Ruth for too long. They thought her muscle was big enough to take on even professionals.

Well, it wasn't. Sam Goose almost hoped some of Mama Ruth's boys would show up tonight. They were going to have to go sooner or later, so why not now instead of having to chase them all over the District?

Somebody was coming up the street. Sam Goose faded into the shadows and watched the approaching figure. Before long he could see that it was a woman. A little bit later, he could see she was young, and the kind a man wouldn't kick out of bed.

Then she turned into the alley, which didn't make a whole lot of sense for a young woman alone at night in this turf. Maybe she had some reason for going by Mama Ruth's back door that didn't have anything to do with Sam Goose.

It wouldn't hurt to find out. At least it wouldn't hurt Sam Goose. Whether it would hurt the woman was up to her.

BOLAN SPENT less than half an hour covering his tracks from Falls Church. He was an expert at it. The best evidence for this was that he was still alive. He also doubted that the three men he'd taken out could have contacted their boss before they died.

It also didn't hurt that in the small hours of a weekday morning, Bolan practically had the streets to himself. Anyone trying to tail him would have stood out like a flashing neon sign.

In fact Bolan was on the lookout more for local police than for drug tails. Suburban police could be paranoid about armed strangers wandering around at night. Bolan didn't want to waste his time or Brognola's in another argument with well-intentioned officers.

The public transportation system had long since stopped running. Walking, running, twice grabbing a passing taxi, Bolan zigzagged across Washington's Virginia suburbs to a reliable all-night car rental establishment near the Pentagon. There he rented a dark blue Firebird, which wouldn't stand out.

Within two hours of the shootout at the Metro station, Bolan was on his way back into Washington to pick up Mama Ruth.

CLAIRE BROUSSON SPOTTED the man before he'd taken three steps out of the shadows. He was built like a basketball player, she noticed, and walked like an athlete. He also sported a well-worn jacket that could conceal a small arsenal.

Brousson was in civilian clothes, but her Chief's Special still rode snugly in its holster on her hip. She also carried a backup gun, a Mini-22, in her bra.

The police sergeant had used lethal force only once in her life, a life that nearly ended when the man she shot was trying to get her gun away from her. After that she made sure that she always had a backup weapon.

There were departmental regulations about that sort of thing, of course. There were also situations where you could either die by the regulations or live to be charged with violating them. Claire knew which choice she would make, if it came down to it.

The stranger was moving faster now. Claire didn't change her pace or turn, but rather tilted her head so she could follow the man with her peripheral vision.

He was in her range of fire now. If he drew, she wanted to be with him.

The man was definitely coming on now. He moved so fast that he went through the edge of the light from a rear window, instead of around it in the shadows. And she could see him clearly.

His face was long and thin, like the rest of him. The man's left eyebrow was missing, and from the corner of the left eye up into the hairline was a ragged raised scar.

Sam Goose.

The match was perfect. It couldn't be anybody but Calvin Pitts's usual partner—the partner of Deacon Whaley's top gun.

The would-be drug king of D.C. had one of his best people here tonight. There could be only one reason for that, too. And at the thought Claire Brousson was tempted to draw her weapon and blast the man on the spot.

Training stopped her. Training, and the thought that if she sucked the man in she might take him alive.

Then whatever Whaley was planning tonight might go down the drain, and she'd have a prisoner as well.

She also knew that Goose had never been prosecuted for any of the five murders everyone knew he'd committed. He'd spent less time in jail for all of them together than some people got for a single drunk-driving conviction.

If she arrested him tonight, he'd be out on the streets again in weeks, if not days. But if she turned him over to Pollock, he might have his own ways of dealing with people the law and its uniformed servants weren't able to touch.

Claire Brousson stopped. She reached into the pocket of her jeans and pulled out a bunch of keys, then pretended to fumble with them. That gave Goose the time he needed to catch up with her.

"Hi, baby. Workin' late?"

"You could say that."

"Matter of fact, I just did. But all work and no play makes Jill a dull girl."

"I don't think I'm *that* dull."

Claire tried to sound interesting without sounding interested. Goose had a reputation for needing to rough up a woman before he had her. She didn't plan to spend much time finding out, but if he had that weakness she could use it against him.

Goose looked her up and down. "I'd say you're one Grade-A fox, if anyone asks me."

"I didn't ask you, but thanks for the kind words."

"Only words?"

Claire shifted so that her body would shield her draw. "There's no way I get hot enough to do it out here. Be reasonable, man."

"Oh, I can be more than reasonable, if you don't mind somebody else's place."

"Anybody I know?"

"Maybe, maybe not. I'm a friend of a lady called Mama Ruth. Least that's what they call her around here."

Claire knew in the next moment that her eyes had betrayed her. Goose's hands danced as he drew both a snub-nosed Colt Agent and a knife.

The policewoman's turn was as fast as Goose's hands. By the time she'd finished her turn, she'd also finished her draw. Her .38 was at waist level, which reduced accuracy, but at a range of two feet she didn't need much.

A wild knife slash tore her shirt and the skin under it. But her two rounds ruined Sam Goose's heart and lungs before he could raise his Colt. His dying reflexes sent a bullet hurtling at her, missing her body but completely wrecking her radio.

Goose lay sprawled on his back in the alley as Claire climbed Mama Ruth's back stairs. The older woman took one look at the police sergeant, then whirled and ran for the telephone.

Claire raced after the woman and caught her as she picked up the telephone.

"No, Mama Ruth! I don't need a doctor."

"Let me be the judge of that, girl."

"Let me tell you what's just happened."

"I'll listen on one condition. You shuck off that blouse and let me work on what hurt you. Did I hear some shootin' just now?"

"You did." By the time Mama Ruth was through giving expert first aid, Claire had finished her story. The older woman nodded.

"Figured it might come to that. Well, I've got me an old shotgun I know how to handle."

"Mama Ruth, when Whaley's men show up they'll be a junior-sized army. Ten shotguns won't be enough."

"How about ten men? I think the boys'll be happy to hear they've finally got a chance—"

"They won't have a chance in hell against Whaley's professionals!"

"Girl, there's no cause to swear like that. Now you just sit tight while I make a couple phone calls."

Everything in Claire's experience screamed at her to grab Mama Ruth and drag her out of the apartment. Everything she knew about the woman told her just as plainly that she wouldn't budge. She wouldn't run from any fight she thought she could win, because she'd lived that way since she was a girl in Kingston. The least Claire Brousson could do was stay and make the fight a little less hopeless.

Mama Ruth was in the middle of the third call when the line went dead. She looked at the policewoman.

"Claire, maybe you have a point after all. Get your shirt on, and I'll get the shotgun."

Two minutes later they learned they were not only cut off, they were also trapped. Four men had the alley covered, and a quick look from the roof showed five more in front.

"Claire, any way we can warn the boys? Nine of those boneyard birds might be more than they can handle."

Claire shook off a grim thought—the bullet that punctured her radio had killed her after all. It would just take her a little longer to die.

"If we could start a fire—"

"There's maybe five, six babies in this building, girl. I won't be hurtin' them."

Claire began to understand why Mama Ruth and Pollock got along so well. Both of them had the same kind of leashed strength and the same care about un-leashing it where innocent people might be hurt.

But innocent people might die tonight no matter what anybody did, unless there was somebody who could bring off a miracle. Whaley's people weren't the kind to leave witnesses around.

Claire shook off that thought too and checked her weapons. Her hands were shaking when she looked over Mama Ruth's old Ithaca 12-gauge. A rat in a trap had the right to be a little bit nervous.

But then it's precisely when he knows he's in a trap that a rat turns to fight.

11

Bolan parked several blocks from Mama Ruth's home and covered the rest of the distance on foot. He would have preferred a blacksuit, but a turtleneck and dark slacks hid him almost as well, even if they lacked pockets.

He didn't miss the Weatherby. Tonight a long-range firefight would be on the menu only if lots of things went wrong. Too many things for Mama Ruth to survive. Maybe even more than the Executioner could handle.

His combat alertness triggered the first warning, when he saw two men standing in a doorway. A second glance told him that they were both armed and one of them was watching Mama Ruth's building.

He managed to get a clear view of the street without alerting the two men. The view turned up two more, also unmistakably part of a stakeout. If these people were smart, they'd have somebody out in back, too. Possibly more "somebodies" than the Executioner could handle quietly.

Any noise he made before he had Mama Ruth on the way to safety was trouble.

An end run took him to the back of the alley. It was staked out, too, with another quartet. Two of them were bending over a man's body. Score for the good guys, or the bad guys? It didn't matter. If anybody had scored at all, the bad guys would be even more alert than usual.

Weapons primed and ready, he crept into the alley. He crawled from one patch of shadow to another, then finally squatted behind a garbage bin to watch and listen. A fifth man had joined the four. Bolan thought he recognized Calvin Pitts.

There was an easy shot at Pitts, but that would alert the others. A death sentence for Pitts could also be one for Mama Ruth.

So, how to quietly get up to Mama Ruth's? The buildings along the alley seemed to be nestled cheek by jowl. With no more than a little luck, the warrior knew that he should be able to cross the roofs.

Bolan uncoiled from his position and pulled himself up silently onto the first landing on a flight of back stairs. From there it was a quick trip to the roof.

Crossing five roofs in four minutes, the warrior had the high ground to himself. Below lay an opponent who apparently hadn't considered that there *was* high ground.

Once Mama Ruth was safe, they were going to get a quick and expensive lesson in tactics. It was unlikely that they would live and learn, but they would live long enough to know that they weren't the undisputed masters of the night streets.

The next building was Mama Ruth's. By a stroke of luck Bolan was able to identify her apartment. Claire Brousson was sitting just within the warrior's angle of vision.

The space between the two buildings was too wide for Bolan to cross easily. He lowered himself from the cornice down to the same floor in the building under him, then whistled softly.

Mama Ruth's head snapped around. So did the muzzle of a shotgun. Claire snatched up her revolver. Then both women smiled.

Bolan pointed at the window and made a lifting gesture with his free hand. Claire gripped the sash and heaved. The window rose a foot at most, then jammed with an alarming screech of strained wood. No dice.

He'd just decided to see if he could shift over when he heard footsteps below. Looking down, he saw that he had company. In another moment he'd have an audience, and he was in a precarious position for firing a weapon. But the chance to cut down the odds was too good to miss. Bolan braced himself as well as he could, then let the Beretta's muzzle drop until it was pointed almost vertically downward.

The warrior snapped off a shot, and a 9 mm tumbler drove into the top of a hardman's skull, ending its journey somewhere around his heart. He was dying as he fell, dead by the time he was at his friend's feet.

The second man flung himself toward the alley. Bolan got off another round, but the angle was bad. It gouged brick, and shifting his aim made his own balance precarious.

No way to go now but down or forward. Bolan chose forward. Before his feet slipped entirely Bolan flung himself at Mama Ruth's window, arms crossed over his face. The sound of shattering glass drowned out the shouts from the alley and the sound of an approaching car.

CALVIN PITTS WASN'T an analytical man at the best of times. His tactics came from the guts and street smarts, not from formal training.

His guts were in more turmoil than usual over the death of another Deacon gunner. Sam had been a good right hand when the shooting started and the closest thing to a friend Pitts had. Sam had also been one of the few people he trusted to guard his back, even against Deacon Whaley.

So Pitts was already considerably upset when things started happening. He heard a shattering window and a car pulling up in front of the building. Right away, he decided that his people had jumped the gun, moving in before he was inside to support them.

Maybe they had good reason. If another gang had sent in a carload of guns and took out Mama Ruth, they'd make a lot of points. Maybe even enough to let them get away with wasting a couple of the Deacon's men.

Either way Pitts looked at it, he and his men didn't belong in the alley.

"Move it!" Pitts whispered. The others would probably think he was being smart by being quiet. The real reason for whispering was that the thought of the big man lying in wait like a spider up there made his throat dry.

BOLAN TOOK MOST of the window and part of the sash with him in his dive. Glass scattered all over the room like grenade fragments, and Mama Ruth yelped as one piece skewered her arm. Claire didn't get any glass, but she threw a horrified look at Bolan as he stood up, his hands bloody.

"Looks worse than it is," he said, knowing that a half dozen superficial cuts could make a man look as if he was bleeding to death. None of the cuts was serious. The worst they might do was make his hands slippery and affect his shooting, particularly with the heavy-kicking Desert Eagle.

That could be bad enough, though. "Anybody got something to wrap my hands?" he asked. Mama Ruth came up with a roll of gauze.

Bolan didn't have time to grab it. Feet thundered on the stairs, so many that the Executioner could only guess at the number of men, and they were coming up both front and back. If they were all bad guys, things were about to get a little hairy.

From the front stairs somebody let off three quick rounds. This got a scream, some answering shots and a lot of shouting from the floor below. It didn't tell Bolan a lot: some of the people coming up the front might be good guys, or they might just have mistaken friends for enemies. A lot of that happened in firefights.

Bolan decided to add to the bad guys' confusion and maybe reduce his own. He nodded to Claire and Mama Ruth. "Stay put, and stay under cover if you can. Don't let anybody you don't recognize through that door."

The older woman nodded. "No problem." She reached into her purse and pulled out a handful of shotgun shells, a full reload for the Ithaca, and put them on the bedside table. Claire put a Mini-22 beside them.

The warrior plunged through the door, nearly taking it off its hinges. He also slammed it hard onto the man on guard, who went down. He held onto his gun, though, was rolling over to aim at Bolan when the Beretta got in the first and last word, chugging out a burst of 9 mm tumblers.

Two gunners stood at the head of the stairs and spun as Bolan took out their friend. Then at least a dozen bullets climbed the stairs from below.

The two men shot at Bolan, but they both had short-barreled .38s—not much for snap shooting at more than six feet. Also, they were both slightly upset at being caught between two fires.

None of the .38 rounds went anywhere near Bolan. His 9 mm reply also missed, but not because he'd suddenly lost his shooting eye. Hands slippery with blood didn't help. Neither did a blast of rounds from downstairs, which sent both hardmen diving for the floor.

Bolan ducked back into the apartment as the two men opened up with more accurate fire. Being a standing target for prone marksmen was pushing his luck. The marksmen instead found their standing targets in Calvin Pitts and his men, who had reached the head of the stairs.

The Executioner listened to the confusion and its results for three seconds before he decided to take advantage of it. He threw the door open and stepped to one side so that Mama Ruth and Claire also had clear targets.

There were plenty to go around. Three of Pitts's men went down in five seconds. One of them had three 9 mm tumblers in his chest, another was severely disfigured after a round of double-ought buckshot hit him in the face and the third was dying from a couple of .38 Specials in the throat.

Calvin Pitts didn't join the casualty list only because the other three got on it ahead of him. He had a clear field of fire at the two men at the other end of the hall. Then he recognized them, just as some of Mama Ruth's boys came clumping up the stairs behind the hardmen.

More noisy confusion. The two men jumped up and ran to Pitts, so fast that even a shotgun blast only nicked one of them. Then all three hurled themselves down the back stairs.

Mama Ruth stood in the hall, aiming at the men coming up the stairs. She was so shaken she didn't recognize her own people. Bolan had a clearer head and recognized Louis. He struck the barrel of the Ithaca up as she fired. The double-ought blew the light and a lot of plaster out of the ceiling. Then Claire was out with the others, wrestling the scattergun away from the older woman.

After a moment, her hands went limp and she sat down, ignoring the plaster, glass and dead bodies. She closed her eyes and started rocking back and forth, crooning something soft and eerie.

"She's callin' the spirits, I think," Louis said.

"Well, I'm more worried about the bodies of any bad guys who got clear," Claire said. "Particularly if they're carrying guns. Any of you people hurt?"

"Joseph's hurt bad and the Fisherman's hurt a little."

By the time Claire had completed first aid on the friendly casualties, Mama Ruth had finished talking to the spirits. Bolan wondered if they'd said anything in reply. One look at the older woman's face told him that he wasn't going to find out.

Another carload of friendlies arrived about two minutes later, which gave enough hands to help with the casualties and enough firepower to discourage any counterattacks.

At least there'd be enough firepower if Bolan was supporting them. Mama Ruth's boys weren't complete novices when it came to firefights, but they had a lot to learn. Lessons that Deacon Whaley's hardmen would teach them in the hardest way.

If the Jamaican vigilantes stayed a long way from the next few fights, Bolan would be a whole lot happier. Keeping the Vietnamese at arm's length was enough of a headache.

Mama Ruth and friends were clear of the area before the police arrived. Claire Brousson bandaged the Executioner's hands and listened to his suggestions about what to do next.

"I can't ride herd on all these crazy island boys," she said finally. "But I can get Mama Ruth up to Chicago before the department notices I'm not where I ought to be. I've got a cousin who has an in with a couple of aldermen. They can improvise a safehouse there."

"If they're not on the take themselves," Bolan pointed out.

"Do you have any better suggestions?"

For once Bolan didn't. Using the D.C. safe apartment for Mama Ruth would make waves, even for a couple of days.

Meanwhile, Deacon Whaley was now down another six or seven men. That might make him pull back, regroup and generally make himself a sitting target. If he sat long enough, some of the other bosses might decide to go for a piece of his drug action, not to mention his hide.

12

Bolan's report of his night's work wasn't the best way to start Hal Brognola's day.

"How's Mama Ruth?"

"Clear," Bolan replied. That one-word answer meant that she was safe for now. It also meant that the Executioner wasn't sure he was on a secure line, and that nobody official should know about how the woman got out of D.C.

"Fine," Brognola said. "I'll pull data for an update on Whaley's bases. I think we're coming up on time to hit them. If we can suck the rest of the Deacon's people into your sights, even better."

Brognola hung up and had time for another cup of coffee before his secretary announced an unscheduled visitor.

A high-ranking CIA man, one of the Company's key people whose identity was virtually nonexistent outside the intelligence community, strode into the big Fed's office. Brognola had talked to him on the phone only two days before, but hadn't seen him for more than a year. The man had lost weight, but not his habit of getting to the point quickly.

"I have an arrangement to propose," he said. "One of your 'people' cooperating with one of ours.

They've already established some cooperation. I want to expand it.''

"Do you want to expand the cooperation? Or is your man putting the heat on you?''

A thin smile told Brognola that he'd scored, but that the other would never admit it. "I see you've had experience with our guy.''

"Enough to know that he's a hard man to turn aside, when he's made up his mind. I take it he has?''

"Yes.''

So, Colonel Phung seriously wanted in on Bolan's war against the Jamaican drug dealers. Brognola had heard worse news. He'd also heard better.

Phung was a loose cannon. His people might be a whole battery of them. They could start the whole business of a Jamaican-Vietnamese war all over again if they wasted the wrong people.

They might also keep the Executioner so busy protecting Helpful Harries that he couldn't watch his own back. Then one of Whaley's hired guns might make the hit of the century.

Brognola bought time to organize his thoughts by offering "Phillips" a cup of coffee.

How much clout did Colonel Phung have with the Company? Probably a lot, if half of what Brognola had heard about the White Tigers' work in their homeland was remotely true.

Not enough, however, to pressure the CIA into approaching Stony Man if it didn't want to. The Company was making this offer on its own. It wanted something, probably a piece of the antidrug action. But it would also need a way around the laws against the CIA operating inside the United States.

The "war against drugs" was vogue. Everybody wanted to score points by being part of it. Getting some of their people experience in domestic crime-fighting operations would make the CIA's role bigger and more effective. Or so somebody apparently hoped.

Brognola grinned. Bargaining and favors were as much a part of intelligence operations as they were of politics. Agencies trying to get a lot and give a little could be as ruthless as an Arab bazaar merchant.

The grin faded. He didn't have time for days of offers and counteroffers. The business had to be settled before Phillips left, which was probably the way the CIA wanted it.

"I think we can deal," Brognola said. "But my man has to be in command."

"No problem."

"He can also limit the number of people you put in the field."

"Fine. He has to let our guy choose them, though."

"I wouldn't have expected anything else," the big Fed replied. Neither the CIA nor Phung would be happy about letting Bolan pick through the files of their men.

"How many were you thinking of sending?" Brognola asked.

Agreeing on how many men the White Tigers ought to send took more time than the rest of the negotiations put together.

They finally agreed on a number and said goodbye with equally cheerful and equally false promises of getting together soon. The CIA man was a widower with grown children, and his social life would make a monk's look like one big party.

Brognola ushered his visitor out with a mental prayer that in order to keep the CIA from dumping on Stony Man, he hadn't dumped too much on Bolan. If the CIA wound up thinking it owed Stony Man a favor, it might be worthwhile. Right now, Brognola knew that he'd at least kept the President from having to referee a brawl between the CIA and Stony Man.

Considering what the President would think of being stuck with that job, maybe it wasn't a small victory after all.

"CALVIN, THIS WAS pretty close to a screwup," Deacon Whaley said. He had the rum bottle and two glasses on the table between himself and Pitts, but the glasses were empty. As badly as he needed one, Pitts wasn't yet desperate enough to grab the bottle and pour himself a drink. With the Deacon in this mood, he needed both hands free.

"We scared Mama Ruth and wasted some of her boys," Pitts replied. "That's what you told me to do, or pretty near."

"I told you to put Mama Ruth on a slab," Whaley said sharply. "Scared isn't dead, not with that old witch."

"Scared is maybe not telling her boys what to do next. Most of 'em won't know to wipe their own asses if she shuts up."

"Yeah, and some of them do. Our friend who blew away a lot of our people might teach the others."

Whaley looked at Pitts for a moment that seemed to stretch into years. Pitts made mental bets on where the Deacon was keeping his iron, and wondered if he'd live to know which one was correct.

Then Whaley lifted the bottle, held it over a glass and poured a healthy shot of the golden-brown rum.

"Ease up, Calvin. I'm thinking we aren't going to get anywhere fast unless we take out the big man." He pushed the glass across the table at Pitts, who managed to pick it up nonchalantly. He emptied it in a single gulp.

"This is just an idea, boss. If it doesn't work any better than some of my others, you can have my ass on a platter."

"I don't have a platter that big. So talk."

Pitts outlined a plan for using the decoy strategy they'd tried before, but on a larger scale. Four or five houses, each ready to ambush the big man when he moved in on them. A radio net, too, linking the houses, so that the firepower could be shifted around as fast as the big man seemed to move.

"Sooner or later we'll get lucky. This guy isn't bulletproof, and he doesn't have spirit warnings." Under the table, Pitts made a gesture for avoiding bad luck. He hoped he was right.

"No problem, except one," Whaley said. "We're short of people. So let's bring the Kingdom and Black Crabs in on this. Let them—what do the Mafia say?— make their bones with us."

That would add at least a dozen more or less reliable gunners, Pitts knew. But it would spread the reliable Deacons pretty thin.

"Don't worry about that," Whaley said, when Pitts raised that objection. "I've got some friends who owe me a few favors. They'll pay up, and when they pay, we'll have all the help we need. Or close to it, anyway."

That was all Whaley would say.

THE KNOCK ON THE DOOR made Bolan draw his .44. He was in a corner with the Desert Eagle aimed at the door when he spoke.

"Who is it?"

"Dragon's Tooth," a soft voice replied.

Bolan unlocked the door without leathering the .44. "Dragon's Tooth," was Colonel Phung's code name for this operation, and probably secure. "Probably" had killed too many men for Bolan to rely on it completely, though.

It was Colonel Phung, with Sergeant Chuyen and another Viet bodyguard who looked just as tough as Chuyen. He also looked too young to have had much combat experience in Vietnam. They were there for the briefing.

"May we enter?" Phung said. His courtesy was so formal it was almost sarcastic.

"Grab a chair and a beer." Bolan pointed to the small refrigerator in the corner of the hotel room. He was willing to observe Vietnamese etiquette, which called for at least a few minutes of refreshments and polite conversation before getting down to business. That would give him a chance to see how Phung—and men he trusted enough to make bodyguards—handled liquor.

If any of them drank too much or talked too loudly, it would take more than the CIA to make him work with Phung. The Executioner wanted only sober soldiers as guests in his house of war.

All three passed the test, with one beer apiece. It was the colonel who finally ended the polite chitchat with a look at his men. They left, and Bolan followed them to a little lounge that gave them a view of both the elevator and the fire stairs.

No enemy was going to get by them without being spotted. No friendly was going to spot their weapons, either, unless he was looking very carefully. Chuyen even had a pack of cards. He and his companion would look as if they were killing time while waiting for a friend.

So far so good, and Bolan said as much when he returned to the room.

"I am glad that you think I can choose bodyguards," Phung said. This time the sarcasm was unmistakable.

"I'm sure you can choose more than that," Bolan replied. "So I'm not going to give you orders."

"I thought you were to be in command."

Phung was clearly prepared to obey that order from the CIA. Just as clearly, he'd lost some status with his people by doing so. Bolan was prepared to give back as much of that status as he could without dancing to the CIA's tune.

"Only in the sense that when orders are given, I'll give them. But I'll give as few as possible, and none to your men except through you. Is this acceptable?"

"It is honorable, and wise, as well."

Phung had no problem with the need for "sterile" weapons, untraceable by the D.C. police or even the FBI. Since the colonel could undoubtedly draw on the CIA's arsenal on an even larger scale than before, Bolan hadn't expected this to be a problem.

"We have no time to test your men, and I have no right to study their files," Bolan went on. "Therefore I leave the choice to you. But I have to ask that you choose only combat veterans."

"You think Tho is not a veteran?"

Bolan hid his unease at having his thoughts read. Phung's reputation in intelligence work was clearly well-earned.

"You know as well as I do how many years your homeland has been enslaved to the Communists."

"Yes, but Tho is older than he looks. Also, all his fighting has not been the sort that the American newspapers talk about."

That implied covert operations for the CIA. "I trust your judgment, since you know what is at stake," Bolan said. "As long as the men are qualified, I won't ask questions about their background. Just remember what General Patton said."

"About winning wars by killing the enemy instead of getting killed yourself?"

"I see we think the same way."

"WE'VE GOT HELP on the way down," Whaley said.

Pitts looked up from cleaning his new piece, a Smith & Wesson 10 mm pistol. Shooting off two boxes of ammo had told him it would be a good alternative to both the Magnums and the Colt .45.

"Anybody I know?"

"Not yet, and I've heard he kind of keeps to himself."

"Just one?"

"Bigger Dawkins isn't enough?"

Pitts gripped the pistol tightly and carefully pointed it at the floor. Dawkins was more than enough by himself, and if he was bringing his usual four or five backups...

"Shit," Pitts muttered.

"What?"

"Bad round in the magazine. Good thing I found it before we moved out.

"You'll have time. Bigger's coming with friends, and they'll need a day to learn the turf."

Then the top gun of the New York Jamaicans would be ready to take the field. Take the field—and Calvin Pitts's place once the shooting was over and D.C. was Deacon's turf free and clear.

Pitts wished that he'd kept his mouth shut. If he hadn't suggested a plan that needed more guns, Whaley wouldn't have enlisted Dawkins's help.

He put everything else except cleaning the automatic out of his mind, and after a while he began to feel better. A while after that, he even had the ghost of an idea.

Dawkins was good. *Too* good, he thought, to be taking orders. Or so the rumors said.

Suppose he didn't like taking orders from Whaley any better than he did from the New Yorkers? Suppose he was coming down here to try for a turf of his own?

And suppose Calvin Pitts offered Dawkins a share of D.C. in exchange for turning that gun of his on

Deacon Whaley instead of himself? Of course, Dawkins would have to go soon after that. But that, too, could be arranged.

If it was, Calvin Pitts would be the Jamaican crack king of D.C.

13

The warehouse was walking distance from the Potomac, but far from any main road. It was too old to be economical, too new to be torn down and too far from anywhere to be turned into condominiums for rich lobbyists.

This made it perfect for a drug drop, and the Kingdom gang had been using it for that purpose for several years. The new management of the Kingdom turf apparently saw no reason to change this. Tonight, the Executioner intended to prove to Deacon Whaley that this was a mistake.

Accompanied by Sergeant Chuyen and a tough corporal named Bao, Bolan crouched under the loading dock. It was rusty, filthy and smelled of stagnant water. The mud on the crumbling concrete apron, though, showed fresh tire tracks.

From the river came the sound of an outboard motor whirring like a giant bug, then silence. Something sank into the soft mud of the bank. Bolan heard the rippling hiss of legs churning their way through long damp grass.

Four men took shape out of the darkness, each bent under the weight of a heavy pack, each with a pistol in his hand. Bao patted his M-16, but the Executioner shook his head.

This was Bolan's fourth raid against Whaley's turf in the past two days. The Viets were pulling their weight, and quite a lot of crack was being found and dumped. Whaley's combined gangs had also lost four soldiers and their weapons.

Otherwise Bolan felt as if he were punching empty air. And he knew that Whaley would try to corner him, eventually try an ambush.

The four men stopped just short of the apron. Two sat down in the unpruned bushes. The others dumped their packs and moved out to stand guard. One of them pulled out a Skorpion machine pistol and unfolded the stock.

Bolan and the Viets held their positions. The man with the Skorpion looked toward the warehouse once, but what he didn't see apparently satisfied him. He quickly looked back toward the road.

A few minutes later lights glowed to the south, bobbing and weaving like the headlights of cars on a rough road. Another minute proved that they were exactly that. Bolan looked away to save his night vision, until the cars cut their lights. Moonlight revealed a tan Blazer and a light pickup.

Three men climbed out of the Blazer, one of them big enough to try out for pro football, with a peculiarly flattened nose. The nose triggered a memory in Bolan, but he couldn't match a name with the face.

"Back it up there," the man with the flattened nose said. He pointed at the loading dock.

"What's—"

"Don't make me worry about you askin' too many questions, man. I get worried, you get dead."

"Who the hell—"

"You know who. You know how I operate. Want me to try it on you?"

The questioner apparently didn't. Flat Nose nodded. "Okay. I can tell you there's stuff in the warehouse we don't want sittin' around if the heat comes down. Fair enough?"

Silence.

Bolan wished he'd allowed time for a search of the warehouse before they staked it out. But the Viets had arrived late. By the time everything was sorted out, searching the warehouse was out of the question.

Bolan waited until he heard the van jolt into movement. Then he waited a little longer, until the van was backing toward the loading dock, its rear doors swinging open.

The Executioner leaped, vaulting into the rear of the van. At the same time the Viets darted left and right, to gain clear fields of fire.

"Freeze!"

The ice in Bolan's voice would have done the job, for sensible men. The van's driver and his companion had either strict orders or no sense. The driver's hand darted to the glove compartment, while the other man reached inside his shirt.

The second man died first, as Bolan demonstrated how useless a van's seat back was against .44 Magnum rounds. The man flew forward, dead, smashing into the dashboard and windshield with enough force to crack the glass with his skull.

The driver almost got off a shot. But beating the Executioner when he'd already drawn would take a miracle. It wasn't the hardman's night for miracles. A head shot from the Desert Eagle took him out of play. Tumblers coming in through the windshield from the Viets killed him a second time, and he ended up draped over the steering wheel.

Bolan stayed low as bullets raged overhead, chipping the glass from the frames. M-16s returned fire. The warrior heard shouts and screams, as the Skorpion suddenly stopped firing.

He was still annoyed at the lack of prisoners. He needed someone who could tell him who was leading him on this chase. It could be Deacon Whaley. It could also be somebody using Whaley as a pawn.

An engine rose in pitch and brakes squealed. As the squealing stopped, someone jerked open the van's side door.

With one hand Bolan chopped down at the side of the man's neck. With the other he jerked at the gun hand. The gunner's limp body flew into the vehicle, nearly somersaulting before it crashed down on the scarred metal floor.

Four shots punched into the van's side, grouped so closely that an outspread hand could have covered the holes. If even one of the holes had been three inches lower, the shooter would have collected the bounty on the Executioner.

BOLAN WAS ALIVE and shooting, and so were the Viets. The light pickup bucked and leaped as bullets ruined its tires. One man fell out, and another leaped, rolled and came up running for cover. The Executioner got off a shot, but it missed its target.

Then 5.56 mm rounds from one of the M-16s found the pickup's gas tank. White flame pushed across Bolan's field of vision, destroying his night sight and blocking his view of the road.

At least that would work two ways. Bolan grabbed his unconscious prisoner and rolled him out of the van. Bao swore in both Vietnamese and Chinese as Bolan landed nearly in front of him.

"Two got away," Chuyen said. "The big one and another. Three are out there." He pointed at sprawled bodies around the burning truck.

Two more in the van plus the prisoner made six fewer hardmen who worked for the D.C. area drug lords. The prisoner might be worth the five dead gunners put together, if he talked. Then Bolan could shift to winning by tactics, instead of winning by body count.

The prisoner was moaning and trying to sit up. He looked as if he had a monumental hangover, and he was probably going to have a weeklong headache. He took one look at the Viets and his mouth opened in the beginnings of a scream. His mouth closed again, as Bolan clamped one large hand over it.

"It doesn't matter a lot to me if you're alive or dead," the Executioner said quietly. It was a tone of voice that had chilled the blood of the hardest Mafia hit men. The hardman stopped struggling and stared at Bolan.

"In fact it doesn't matter at all," Bolan went on. "And my friends here would really like to see you dead. They have a debt to pay.

"But we can make a deal. Tell me everything you know about your work in D.C., and you can walk out of here."

The man looked at Bolan's face and found little mercy there. In the Viets' he found even less. Chuyen had drawn his knife and was making delicate passes at the man's groin. The message about how he would die got through.

"I'm down from the Big Apple, with Bigger Dawkins," the man told them. "He came down 'cause Deacon Whaley asked for help."

A lot fell into place with the name "Bigger Dawkins." One of the top soldiers of the Jamaican drug gangs in New York, his appearance on the D.C. scene would have paid a lot of debts to Whaley.

More fell into place as the man went on. A lot of it concerned New York. Bolan's memory worked overtime on the names and places he was learning. But by the time the man ran dry, the Executioner had what he'd been looking for.

Deacon Whaley was going to get a reprieve. Not a pardon, but a few more days of life while Bolan visited New York. On his own Whaley was bad enough. With a New York connection he might strain even the Executioner's resources.

Meanwhile, somebody *was* due a pardon.

"On your feet, mister," Bolan said. "I said if you talked you'd walk. So start walking. Even better, start running. Some of your friends might still be around and wonder why you stayed behind so long."

The thought of meeting a traitor's death gave springs to the man's legs. He leaped to his feet, groaning at the pain in his head and back, then started off toward the river. At twenty yards away he realized he was going the wrong way and retraced his steps, holding his head as if afraid it would fall off.

The light of the burning pickup showed the man clearly, when Corporal Bao snapped up his M-16 and fired three rounds. The man threw up his arms and sprawled onto some scruffy bushes.

Bolan snatched the M-16 out of Bao's hand and threw it on the ground. The man jumped back, out of Bolan's reach, and drew a knife.

"No!" Chuyen shouted, and closed with his comrade, gripping his knife hand. The two Viets struggled for a moment, shouting at each other. Bolan picked up the M-16, snapped on the safety and started to remove the magazine.

He'd just pressed the release when a gun was fired somewhere off to his right. He whirled, seeing Chuyen and Bao falling to the ground. Bolan dived to the pavement as two more bullets whizzed past overhead.

Bao was dead, his skull shattered. Chuyen was wiping blood off his face. When he could see, his own rifle swung toward the warehouse. Bolan grabbed his arm.

"Stay down," he whispered in Vietnamese. "If they think we're dead—"

"Yes."

Another nerve-stretching wait began. Whoever was inside the warehouse might be communicating with the hardmen, calling them back to clean up.

If that happened, it was even odds who'd be cleaning up whom. Bolan set out four grenades, checked the pins, snapped another magazine in the borrowed M-16 and settled down to waiting.

Moments later Bolan saw two darker shadows appear in the door to the loading dock. They made poor targets, and the warrior didn't want to reveal his position by firing.

Bolan pulled the pin, held the grenade for a two-count to make it difficult to throw back and lobbed the bomb onto the loading dock. The two men split as they heard it clatter, and one ran straight into the edge of the door.

He'd just recovered when the grenade went off, the concussion blowing him into the dusty corridors of the warehouse. The second man fell off the loading dock trying to get down. He landed on his knees and withdrew a Beretta 84. For one moment he had a clear shot at the Executioner.

The gunner ignored the opportunity, leaping to his feet and running instead.

Bolan waited just long enough to see which way the hardman was running, then jerked Chuyen to his feet.

"Come on!"

"We can't leave—"

"All right." Bolan hadn't forgotten the Vietnamese respect for their dead.

Bao was light enough that even slung over Bolan's shoulder, he hardly slowed the warrior down. The Executioner and Chuyen were a good eighty yards from the warehouse when it blew.

Up, out, and in every other direction. Where the warehouse had once stood, there was now a ball of flame crowned with chunks of brick, stone and steel.

Then the ball of flame collapsed. The blast thundered past Bolan and his companions, punching them to the ground, hammering their ears. The warrior opened his mouth to equalize the pressure on his eardrums and inhaled a lungful of grit and muck. The heavier bits of warehouse collapsed into a smoking pile, and the lighter bits rained down all around the two men.

The Executioner kept his nose to the ground until he was sure the fireworks were over, then cautiously rose. The concussion had affected even his strong sense of balance. He used the M-16 as a crutch while he brushed muck off the blacksuit with the other hand.

Twenty yards closer to the blast, he would have been unconscious. Forty yards closer, he would have been dead.

But he was alive. What lay dead, buried under the ruins of the warehouse, was any plans Whaley had made for using the arsenal. Bolan wondered if there was enough left for even the best weapons experts to tell who had supplied what.

Wherever he'd got it, Whaley had managed to bring enough into the country to make a major bang. Were his suppliers helping him with that, too?

More questions, and no answers. Not now, anyway, and Bolan intended to leave the job of finding them to Hal Brognola. Stony Man Farm had its own weapons experts and computers that not even the Defense Intelligence Agency could match. They could pick over the warehouse.

Bolan had a date in New York.

"Chuyen, you wait here with Bao. I'll get the car. Then I'll drop you off at the Mekong Flower and you can report to Colonel Phung."

Unlike his late comrade, Chuyen was too good a soldier to disobey orders. But his face wore a puzzled frown as Bolan disappeared into the night.

HAL BROGNOLA HAD a busy two days after he received Bolan's message about the planned side trip to New York.

The Stony Man weapons experts weren't called in to sift the ruins of the warehouse. The DIA and the local police handled that. Brognola still had to stay close to the phone, to make sure that whatever anyone else learned got passed on to him.

With men like Deacon Whaley and the unknown weapons dealers, one could afford very few mistakes of any kind.

For that reason Brognola was too busy to ask for periodic reports from Bolan, even if he'd been in the habit of doing so. He was even too busy to read the papers. However, he did read the morning intelligence digest prepared by Aaron Kurtzman, but it didn't say anything about a sudden outbreak of untimely deaths among Jamaican criminals in New York or anywhere else.

On the third day he got a visit from Bolan.

"You worked fast" was Brognola's only comment.

"I suspect we don't have much time," Bolan replied. "If I was Whaley, I'd be getting desperate. I wanted to make sure that he wouldn't get help from New York, no matter how desperate he got."

"The people you hit weren't the only place he could get help. The CIA has uncovered a Chinese connection."

"If the ChiComs try to make contact, we can leave that to the Company," Bolan said.

"I was thinking about the Triads." The Chinese answer to the Mafia was looming larger on the international crime scene with each passing year.

"Working with Beijing?" Bolan sounded curious rather than skeptical. Both he and the big Fed knew that crime made even stranger bedfellows than politics. And when politics influenced crime . . .

"It wouldn't be the first time they've tried to play both sides of the same game. One hand tries to get their assets out of Hong Kong, the other tries to cover their assets by playing footsie with Beijing."

Bolan frowned. "Maybe the CIA could handle that. It's right up their alley."

"That and a lot of other things that aren't really their business," Brognola grumbled.

"Are they on our case about Phung again?"

"No, Phung's on our case on his own. He wonders if you're telling the truth about Bao's death. He doesn't approve of the man's being kill-crazy, but thinks you might have killed him yourself. He wanted the man alive for White Tiger justice."

"Shall I tell Colonel Phung what to do with his suspicions?"

"No, I will. I can be ruder. You'll have Phung behind you."

"Not if I move in on Whaley right now."

"Striker, that's violating our agreement with the CIA *and* Phung. Getting both of them pissed off won't help put Whaley down. Besides, the Deacon's been keeping a low profile since you went north."

"He can't keep it too long without going out of business," Bolan pointed out.

"He can keep it long enough for Phung to find out, if you go in solo," Brognola said, sighing. "If I said I was happy about this situation, I'd be lying. Suppose I ask the CIA to tell Phung to stop jerking our chain? You have a little talk with the good colonel. If we aren't both satisfied, you can go in solo, when and where you please, and I'll take the heat."

"Fair enough."

"I GOT SOME BAD NEWS and some good news," Deacon Whaley announced.

Calvin Pitts looked at Bigger Dawkins, then at the ceiling. It didn't matter which came first, if neither of them screwed his plans for striking a bargain with Dawkins.

"The bad news is that New York's cutting us off."

"Meaning?" Dawkins asked.

"Seems like our big friend paid your boss a visit. You don't have a boss anymore. He isn't the only one, either."

Dawkins pulled at his misshapen nose. Pitts wondered if that was how it had gotten bent out of shape.

"So?"

"I got to spell it out? The word is that nobody else is coming down here to help us. We fight the man and the Viets with what we've got."

New York had lots of drug action. Also lots of people fighting for a piece of it. In that fight you needed all the soldiers you could get, and ten more besides.

If helping Deacon Whaley meant getting your soldiers and maybe yourself blown away, well, anybody could see the writing on the wall: anyone who helped the Deacon was dead.

Wanting to live to spend their profits, the New York Jamaicans were pulling the plug on Whaley.

"Okay," Dawkins said. "What's the good news?"

"The cutoff doesn't mean you. Word I got, you can stay or go as you please."

To Pitts this didn't seem like such a big favor, considering that Dawkins was probably the senior man left in his gang. Plenty of men could advise him or kill him; nobody could give him orders.

Then Pitts saw the way the Deacon was looking at Dawkins, and decided that Whaley was wrong, that it was bad news all around.

Whaley wanted Dawkins to stay so he could play the New Yorker off against Pitts. That meant the Deacon was right on top of Pitts's idea of offering to split D.C. with the New Yorker if the new man would take out Whaley.

Pitts cursed himself. Whaley couldn't really read minds, but he'd survived too many plots not to recognize the possibility of another one when it came up and slapped him in the face.

In his eagerness Calvin Pitts had forgotten that. A man could die from such eagerness. *Would* die, if Deacon Whaley was satisfied that Dawkins could take over as his number two.

"I'll stay," Dawkins said. "I think our friend's going to be back here before long. This is where we pay him off. I'd like to keep a couple of my best guns with me, too."

"As many as you like," Whaley replied. This time Dawkins looked at Pitts. The younger man tried to

meet the New Yorker's eyes and thought he succeeded.

He knew he'd just received a message. Dawkins
might be a friend, or he might be an enemy. There was
no way he was going to be an easy target.

14

The two opponents got ready for the final confrontation in D.C.

Deacon Whaley cut back his positions to a main base and two outposts. The base was linked to the outposts by CB radio, which Whaley knew could be intercepted. He thought that the verbal code he'd worked out would solve that problem.

He was wrong. With what Bolan had learned from Mama Ruth's informants, Stony Man Farm broke the code within an hour. The Executioner knew exactly where to go and approximately how much time he would have before Whaley's reinforcements arrived.

The warrior was free to spend his time making sure that his own security was better than Whaley's. They had no choice but to take what the CIA could come up with in the way of sterile weapons.

"Do you think the Company's playing games?" Bolan asked after a final weapons inspection.

"I doubt it. Phung and the White Tigers aren't an expendable asset, as far as I can tell. The Company's not set up for in-country work."

Bolan looked around to make sure that none of the Viets were within earshot. "So why did they think it would help to spring the Viets on us at all?"

When Brognola replied, Bolan could hear the weariness in his friend's voice. "The Viets would have dealt themselves in one way or another."

Bolan kept any other reservations to himself.

"Anything you desperately need?" Brognola added.

Bolan mentally reviewed the arsenal. "Not really. The M-16s are old but look good. The Company knew the Viets can't handle 7.62 mm NATO. All the pistols take 9 mm."

"Explosives?"

"We could use a few more grenades. But none of the Viets is a qualified demo man. We won't be able to use more C-4 than I can pack myself. Same with WP."

"All right. Good hunting, Striker."

IN A RENOVATED MANSION on the South Side of Chicago, Claire Brousson was trying to calm Mama Ruth. She couldn't help wondering why the woman had decided to get nervous when she was almost certainly safe.

Safe as long as Rance Pollock was alive and in the field, because he would keep Deacon Whaley too busy to find out where Ruth was, let alone go after her. If that changed, Ruth might be in trouble again.

It was pretty plain to Claire Brousson, however, that Pollock was a man who wouldn't give up unless he was dead. He would also be hard to kill. If he was the man she thought he was, a lot of people had tried, many of them better than Deacon Whaley.

This confidence in Pollock made Claire dig in her heels with Ruth.

"You sure your cousin's straight?" the older woman was asking for the tenth time.

"I wouldn't bet he's any angel. But cheating on liquor licenses and contracts isn't the same thing as selling crack to teenagers. He's got plenty of friends among the police, too. They'll cover anything he can't."

Ruth shook her head. "Guess it's funny, me wondering if I'm safe when I stuck my neck out back in D.C. Maybe I'm getting too old to want to die."

Claire hugged the woman, who had begun to seem almost like a second mother. Her own had died just after Claire joined the police force, worn out by the strain of raising three children without a husband.

"You're too old to waste time worrying about what's not going to happen, that's for sure," Claire said.

"No waste of time, worrying about what's going to happen to you, if you go back to D.C."

"Mama Ruth, we've been over this before. There's no 'if' about it."

"Pollock doesn't seem like a man who needs much help."

"We were handy when he came around, the both of us. Anyway, I wasn't thinking of going out and helping him put Whaley down. I don't have enough vacation time for that. I'm going to go back and keep an eye on what the D.C. police are doing. Anything I do for Mr. Pollock, I'll do through channels."

The words didn't ring true even to Claire, and Ruth was looking at her with a "Don't bullshit *me* girl!" expression on her long face. Claire grinned.

"Okay. I guess it's because I've never walked away from a fight since I was a girl. But I'm really not going to walk into this one unless I can help Rance that way."

"All right, Claire. You do what you think's right. Surely no way I'm going to stop you, even if I said things I wouldn't like to hear said to me."

Moments later Claire left the house, heading for D.C.

IN THE STREET outside the Mekong Flower, the evening shadows were getting long. Periodically Bolan peered discreetly into the street. So far there were no signs that anyone had the place staked out.

It was possible that Whaley had men on the job who were too good for the Executioner to spot. Such men existed, but the warrior doubted that any of them were working for Deacon Whaley. Maybe Bigger Dawkins, the New York enforcer, but he wouldn't be wasted on a stakeout.

In fact Whaley probably wouldn't stick anybody out where he'd be an easy target. The man wasn't a fool. He knew what happened to the men he'd sent out previously. He also knew what would happen to him if too many more of his people didn't come back. He'd be forced to keep his horns pulled in and wait for the enemy to come to *him*.

Bolan could hear metallic clicks from the room next door as the Viets loaded magazines. Bolan wanted five loaded mags for each rifle and four for each pistol. Some of the Viets looked as if they enjoyed using rock 'n' roll—full automatic. They'd shoot themselves dry too soon for Bolan's peace of mind, but he wouldn't have to punish them for it. If Whaley's men didn't get the careless Viets, Phung would.

Bolan still wasn't pleased about having Phung along, but he had to admit that it wasn't entirely the colonel's fault. He'd have resented anyone forced on him by some faceless bureaucrat exerting pressure on Hal Brognola.

Rattling replaced clicking, as the Viets worked freshly oiled bolts to test them. Somebody must have started to jack a round into a chamber, because Bolan heard a blast of Vietnamese. It was Phung, and the Executioner couldn't make out all the words. He didn't need to.

Phung might be riding on Bolan's coattails in this mission, but he'd paid for his ticket. He was a good, professional soldier by any standards. Maybe the D.C. back alleys weren't his favorite battlefield, but he would follow Bolan and be a handy man in any sort of firefight.

Darkness had fallen and Bolan sat on a rickety chair to check his own weapons. He wasn't sure he'd need the Weatherby, but there was a chance, and he wouldn't trust it or its ammo to another man. He had fifteen rounds and the four-power sight for it. The rest of his arsenal included the stocked 93-R, a pouchful of magazines, another pouchful of grenades and sticks of C-4 explosive. A third pouch held magazines for the Desert Eagle.

It was when he started counting the .44 Magnum magazines that Bolan felt a sudden chill. Not the familiar coolness of knowing that the battle was about to start, but rather the sharper coldness of his battle-honed instincts, warning of danger.

One of the magazines contained only six rounds, instead of eight. It showed no signs of tampering, but Bolan knew it had been full when he put it in the pouch. He never used a magazine that wasn't full to capacity, except for the old 20-round M-16 magazine that could jam if loaded with more than eighteen.

Running out of ammunition in the middle of a firefight delighted your enemies and dismayed your friends. That's *if* you had any left by the time you died. Having ammunition disappear mysteriously before the shooting started might not be so fatal, but it wasn't something Bolan liked to see.

Not when he didn't know where the rounds were, who might pick them up, or what the person might do with them.

"Colonel Phung," he called. "I need you."

The colonel appeared wearing tiger-striped camouflage fatigues and a sour look. "What is it that cannot be said before all my men?"

"This." Bolan held out the magazine. Phung's eyebrows rose.

"You delay us for this?"

"This could kill somebody if the rounds are in the wrong hands."

"The wrong hands could have been yours, not putting the rounds there in the first place. Are you trying to find a reason for refusing our help, now of all—"

The colonel broke off at the look on Bolan's face. He took a deep breath. "Forgive me. I meant no insult."

"I wasn't insulted. I just think you were wrong. Wrong as I'd be, ignoring this."

"I know of no weapons among my men that would take the Magnum rounds. Such a pistol would be hard to hide, yes?"

Bolan shrugged. "A search would be impossible. I know the implications of the insult. But I think you and I will have to be careful even before we reach Whaley's headquarters. One of us should be watching the others at all times."

"Except Chuyen. He should watch, not be watched," Phung said briskly.

"We'll hope those two rounds turn up in an enemy's back, not ours," Bolan said. The words didn't ease his own tension, but he saw Phung relax slightly. "How soon can we move out?"

Phung looked at his watch. "Ten minutes?"

"No problem."

CALVIN PITTS WATCHED Bigger Dawkins relieve himself with a sigh. He wasn't sure why for the past hour the New Yorker had been watching him like a snake watching a bird. He wasn't sure he wanted to know, either.

All he wanted was for the shooting to start. Then he could arrange the "accident" for Dawkins with a lot less trouble. Whaley might suspect the worst, but without proof what could he do? Particularly if Pitts scored on their opponent *and* was the only possible number-two man for the ruler of Washington's Jamaican drug gangs?

Not that Deacon wouldn't try to figure out something to do to Pitts. But that would take time, and Pitts might think faster. Then it would be Calvin Pitts bossing the capitol's Jamaicans. Bigger Dawkins wasn't going to be nearly as good for the Calvin Pitts problem as Deacon Whaley thought.

HAL BROGNOLA had decided to have a cat nap on his office sofa, and slept until eleven-thirty, when his radio alarm went off. A message from the CIA had come in an hour before, but enough people knew why Brognola was asleep and were determined not to disturb him.

When Brognola finally read the message, he took a whole minute telling the people who hadn't woken him that they had really stepped in it. Then he punched in a telephone number he'd been given two days earlier.

All he got was an answering machine, with a Vietnamese-accented voice saying "You have reached Son and Thay, Custom Draperies and Blinds. We cannot take your call at the moment, but if you will leave your name, telephone number and a brief message, we will return it as soon as possible."

That told Brognola that Mack Bolan was already on his way to the final confrontation with Deacon Whaley. On his way, and out of reach of any secure communications.

IN SOUTHEASTERN Washington, D.C., a battered dark-blue Ford van pulled into an alley and stopped. Eight men climbed out. One of them was noticeably taller and broader than the others, but they all wore black and all were armed.

"I'll take point," the tall man said. "Chuyen, you take the rear. Colonel, stay within whispering distance of me, please."

That was an order, in spite of the "please." Then he seemed to merge with the darkness as he stepped forward, catfooted and alert, seeking the enemy.

15

Darkness had swallowed the street outside Deacon Whaley's headquarters. Calvin Pitts cleaned his already spotless 10 mm gun and stared at the ceiling. He wished Sam Goose was still with them. Sam always had something funny to say to fight off jitters, his own or a friend's.

Wishing wouldn't bring Sam back. Wishing wouldn't turn Bigger Dawkins into somebody who was fun to have around, either. Pitts leathered his weapon and stretched out until his feet were halfway across the hall.

"Somebody could trip over you, that way," Dawkins said. "Knock out their brains."

Pitts didn't say "That makes you safe," as much as he wanted to. Instead he grinned.

"What's so funny?" Dawkins asked.

"Maybe Mama Ruth's boys'll show up tonight. Then we can blow them away, too. *Nobody* left to argue with us."

Dawkins didn't ask who Pitts meant by "us." Instead he shook his head.

"Maybe. Maybe our friend has some smarts, too. He tells Mama Ruth's boys 'wait until Deacon whistles up his friends. Then you take them while I take the Deacon.' ''

"Those boys Mama Ruth lined up, they couldn't ambush an old folks' picnic."

"Maybe they've been learning," Dawkins said. The slide on his Star .45 went home with an angry snick.

"Who from?"

"One guess."

"You really think this guy's Batman?"

"No. Batman doesn't use guns. Our friend throws more lead than a rifle squad. At least that's what you've been telling me."

Before Pitts could resent the hint of lying, Dawkins shrugged. "Deacon says so, too. I figure you both can tell your ass from a hole in the ground. So this guy could be doin' damned near anything."

"You always so cheerful, Bigger?" Pitts asked.

"Beats bein' dead."

BOLAN LED the seven Vietnamese along a winding route, through alleys, parks and vacant lots, toward Deacon Whaley's headquarters. He figured they would be spotted sooner or later, but the later the better.

He also intended to keep the assault force together as long as possible. They'd surely wind up separated into two or three teams when the firefight opened. Right now, though, Bolan wanted everyone where he could keep an eye on them. If anybody had those Magnum rounds, he might make a mistake and give the Executioner a clue.

Some people, and not all of them primitive, thought Mack Bolan had supernatural powers. He didn't, but at the moment the warrior would have given anything for five minutes of Superman's X-ray vision. Then he'd scan the men with him to see if anyone was carrying the missing .44s and a weapon to fire them.

Bolan turned his mind back to the job at hand. They'd cross the next vacant lot and be in the alley that led to the back of Whaley's house.

No sign of any sentries this far out. Any closer in and it would be better to take them out silently. For a backup the Desert Eagle would be better than the Weatherby. Enough range and a one-hit knockdown punch, plus less danger of hitting innocents a block away.

Bolan drew and raised the massive .44, checking the sights. Behind him he heard boots crunch lightly on a patch of gravel, then a wordless mutter that might have been in any language.

A thunderclap blast and eye-searing muzzle-flash caught Bolan in midstride. He was already going down as Colonel Phung cursed. The Executioner landed rolling, coming up with a round in his pistol's chamber.

He snapped off the safety as he saw the spectacle at the tail of the line. Chuyen was wrestling with another Vietnamese, trying to immobilize the man's hands without hurting him.

One of those hands held something that gleamed dully in the faint streetlights, like a blue-finished gun. A small gun, but unmistakably it had just fired one of the missing .44s at Colonel Phung.

Then the Vietnamese gunman jerked free, falling over backward as he broke Chuyen's grip. Both hands were coming up now, and the dull gleam was swinging toward Bolan. The Executioner's finger tightened on the Desert Eagle's trigger.

But standing over the Viet and raising the butt of his M-16 Chuyen was blocking Bolan's shot. Bolan's mouth opened to order Chuyen clear, but the pistol in the fallen man's hand spoke with more authority.

Climbing almost vertically, the .44 slug hit the point of Chuyen's jaw. It removed most of the man's head above the nose. Even Bolan felt his stomach twitch at the sight of his former ally.

Chuyen's falling corpse blocked the man's next shot. Before the Viet could move, Bolan was on him. A boot to the man's temple stretched him out, limp and motionless. Bolan crouched to see if he was still breathing.

He hoped so, as much as the man deserved to die. They needed him alive, to learn what lay behind his treachery. What—and if possible, *who*.

For a minute it wasn't clear that either the Viet or Bolan would stay alive. The rest of the force surrounded them, fingers on triggers. The Viets didn't say much, but they didn't have to, to get their message across.

They wanted the man who sought Colonel Phung's life and took that of their friend Chuyen, or they were going to attack Bolan.

It took more than an attempt on his life to upset Colonel Phung. He stormed in among his men, ordering them back to their posts and on the alert.

"We are in more danger now because of this madman who took our enemies' pay. We will be dead if you are all as foolish as he was."

The same loyalty to Phung that had made the Viets ready to kill Bolan made them obey. They faded into the night, while Phung knelt beside Bolan and helped him bind and gag the unconscious prisoner.

"Why?" the colonel said. Much of his arrogance seemed to have died with Chuyen. He sounded calm but honestly confused.

"I don't know. That's why I wanted this guy alive. But I can tell you how."

Using the point of his combat knife thrust into the muzzle, Bolan held up a 2-shot American Derringer Model 1.

"The only really concealable weapon that takes the .44 Magnum round. He must have had it loaded with the stolen rounds and ready to draw. When he saw me with the Desert Eagle, aimed generally in your direction, he must have decided this was the time. Even if only one man thought I had done it, he could have shot before I realized I was suspected of murdering you."

Phung cursed, then shook his head. "But why steal the ammunition? Had he never heard of ballistic tests? They would have shown that a weapon other than yours fired the round. How stupid can a man be?"

"You've been a soldier long enough to know the answer to that one," Bolan said wearily. "Maybe he hadn't heard of ballistics tests. Or maybe he thought that if somebody heard you were killed with a .44 Magnum round, they would come after me right away. That's assuming somebody didn't blow me away on the spot."

"Well, all his plans are dead, and he will join them when we have learned what he knows."

"We paid a price, though," Bolan said, looking at Chuyen's body. Somebody had covered the mangled head with a scarf, now crimson with blood.

"We have not long to wait before paying Chuyen's debt," Phung said. He knelt again, muttering what sounded like both a prayer for Chuyen and a solemn curse on his enemies. Then he rose.

"Let us hide the bodies as best we can and move on. If our enemies are not deaf, they will be alert."

In his eagerness to avenge Chuyen, Phung seemed ready to act without waiting for Bolan's input. Right now, though, he was doing exactly what Bolan would have suggested.

Within a minute they had the body and the prisoner bound and gagged out of sight in a clump of weeds. Then Bolan fell in at the rear of the line, Phung took point and they moved out.

THE MEN WAITING at Deacon Whaley's headquarters weren't deaf, and they were alert. Calvin Pitts found Bigger Dawkins at the head of the basement stairs, when he came up from radioing to the outposts.

"They're comin' in?"

"Fast as they can roll."

"You warn them about ambushes?"

"The police won't have time—"

"I wasn't thinkin' police, Calvin."

"Still thinkin' our friend's got friends?"

"Haven't proved he hasn't, one way or another. You know what I think's safest."

Pitts had warned the reinforcements from the outposts to be alert, because the police were likely to be a bit nervous by now. He figured that if the sentries kept an eye out for the police, they'd spot anything else in time.

If they did walk into a police trap, of course, that would be a bad deal. In that case it wouldn't make a hell of a lot of difference if the big man had friends or not. The fight would stay between the people who were already here, and the Deacons would just have to do their best.

It would have to be good enough, too, or they were going to be seriously dead before morning. In his gut Calvin Pitts knew that this was the last round of the fight. It could only end when the big man—or the Deacon gang—was gone.

Calvin Pitts pulled a box of 10 mm Magnum shells from the cedar chest in the front hall and stuffed another dozen rounds into the pockets of his jacket. Thinking that Bigger Dawkins might be right didn't help Pitts's mood. But if the man was, then extra ammo *would* help.

AT POLICE HEADQUARTERS Claire Brousson grabbed a cup of coffee and a doughnut on her way to her locker. When she came back armed and in uniform, she looked at the call log. Nothing that could be Rance Pollock in action showed up.

Because this was an extra shift for her, she really didn't have to stay. Reason told her that Pollock was a creature of the night, because the men he fought feared daylight. The more duty she pulled at night, the better for Pollock.

Her pistol was spotless, but there were always shotguns that needed cleaning. After the shotguns there were papers to file, bulletins to post and other jobs to invent if she had to. She'd rather scrape chewing gum out of wastebaskets with her fingernails, then go off-duty while the big man might be out there facing Deacon Whaley.

IN A DRIVEWAY in northeastern D.C., a V-6 engine rumbled to life. Coughing asthmatically, a Chevrolet van backed out into the street. Rackham was at the wheel, Louis in the back and four other young men squatted on the floor.

Word on the streets was that it was all coming down on Deacon Whaley. He and the others weren't about to sit home hoping to hear about what went down on the nightly news.

Besides, Louis wasn't going to stick himself or his people right into the shooting. Especially not the first time he was leading them, since Mama Ruth moved him up ahead of Rackie. They'd come in, see what was happening and find a good place to move in before they actually *did* anything.

As the van swung on to New York Avenue, Louis was sure that even Mr. Pollock would approve of that kind of thinking.

16

Whaley had posted sentries around his headquarters by the time Bolan covered the last hundred yards. This didn't slow the attack much, but it did considerably speed up the sentries' deaths.

Bolan took one from behind, wrapping his arm around the man's neck and slashing the combat knife across the guy's throat with the other. Then he collected the mini-Uzi and let the body sprawl on pavement.

The other sentry sold his life dearly, or at least noisily. Sergeant Tho who took him out had a silencer on his Beretta, but a silencer wasn't enough against an alert opponent. Particularly not when the first shot wasn't a kill.

The Jamaican reeled backward, raising a Ruger Security Six with one hand and clapping the other against his bloody thigh. His three shots missed the Viet, but Tho killed the Jamaican on his second try. But the alarm was raised.

Bolan heard shouts and running feet as at least two other sentries shifted position. The Viets opened fire, but none of the rounds found a target.

Phung and Bolan shouted for a cease fire. That gave a marksman high in the target building the delusion that *he* had a target.

The hardman was closer to being right than Bolan cared for. Tumblers drilled past the Executioner's ears and whined off the pavement near his feet.

In that kind of situation standard infantry tactics called for "suppressive fire," which meant filling the air around the marksman with lead in the hope of encouraging him to miss or even duck.

But this wasn't a standard infantry situation. Bolan studied the house, drew two more rounds, then chose less orthodox tactics.

Propelled by a long muscular arm, a grenade arched toward the house. It crashed through the window in the back door, knocking out most of the glass. The rest of the glass and the door itself vanished when the grenade exploded.

Then Bolan grabbed for the two nearest Viets as they started to rush forward. One of them glared at him. The other managed to put his question into words.

"Why not rush them now?"

"That's what they'll be expecting. They'll be ready for us. Sooner or later they'll wonder why we don't come in. Then they'll get nervous or curious. Maybe both. At least then some of them will come out."

The gunners might not come out the door. They might even try to outflank Bolan. If they did, Bolan would move into the house, clean out the men still inside and hold it against its former occupants.

Either way, the Deacons would have to move through the sights of men waiting for them.

The waiting went on, until Bolan's skin began to prickle from anticipated danger. Maybe not life-or-death, but this gang lying low didn't smell right. Were their reinforcements closer than he'd expected?

Before Bolan could answer his own question, a whisper in Vietnamese and a pointing finger drew his eyes to the roof of the house. A dark-clad figure had climbed out of a dormer window and was sliding across the roof toward the shelter of a chimney. Bolan raised the Weatherby, using the sight in place of binoculars.

The man looked unarmed, but he had a small radio and what had to be a flare pistol stuck in his belt. A lookout, but looking out for what? For reinforcements already moving in to take Bolan from the rear.

The Executioner nearly used the Weatherby right then. Being short a lookout would mess up Whaley's plan nicely. It would also warn the Deacons that the attackers knew about the trap. Then they might pass the warning on to their friends.

Bolan was going to see if the trap could be turned against the trappers.

He lowered the Weatherby, made sure he could keep track of the lookout with the naked eye and squatted on the pavement. The two Viets looked at him with a mixture of curiosity and impatience. One of them made a magical sign; the other shook his head.

Bolan wasn't going to consult spirits or anybody else about the outcome of the fight. He knew what would happen if Whaley's reinforcements came in making nice targets of themselves. Once they were down, it would be a straight fight between Bolan's men and whoever was in the house.

CALVIN PITTS CROUCHED by the radio and listened to the lookout reporting.

It looked as if the whole attack was coming in from the rear. Not smart, but maybe they weren't really as strong as they needed to be.

"That could be why they didn't follow up the grenade," Dawkins said.

"Scared of losing people?" Whaley asked.

"Wouldn't be the first, last or only."

Pitts saw Whaley frown at the New Yorker's tone. Neither of them liked Dawkins's way of making like he was the only one who knew anything about a shootout. Maybe he knew more than Calvin Pitts, but Pitts wouldn't even bet on that.

He was, however, going to stay alive to make that bet. That meant not getting into a fight with friendlies. "We can send somebody out to count heads, if Laro doesn't do the job."

"Not comin' in the back door doesn't mean they're not watchin' it," Whaley replied. "Anybody we send out, he goes out the front door and loops way around before he hits the alley."

"How about we send three, maybe four?" Pitts asked.

"Maybe, if you tell them and tell us why," Dawkins said.

Whaley glared at the New Yorker. "Calvin stays here. I can't lose him."

"You want me to go?"

"If it's going to hurt the people out there so much, why not?"

Pitts shifted sideways, to have extra room for a quick draw. From the look on Dawkins's face, he thought he might need it real soon.

Then from the front they heard an engine shift down and stop. A car door clanged, and the radio squawked.

"We got some people comin' out of a van in the street. They look like—I'll be damned if—"

Laro's words ended in a burst of gunfire.

THE GUNFIRE SURPRISED Bolan even more than it did Calvin Pitts. He wasn't too surprised, however, to see the lookout draw a pistol and fire down into the street in front of the house. Then the lookout raised his flare pistol.

The flare never went off. A Magnum slug from the Weatherby hurled the man off the roof. He screamed briefly, but any noise he made landing was lost in the din of the firefight raging on the other side of the house.

"Come on!" the warrior shouted, up now and running toward the back door of the house.

The Viets' instincts to close and kill kept them from questioning Bolan's sudden change of tactics. In any case the Executioner hadn't changed the tactics, only altered them as the situation required.

An enemy, or somebody the Deacons thought was an enemy, was out in front. And with an enemy in their sights inexperienced troops tended to forget about flanks and rear. Bolan didn't think Bigger Dawkins was enough to make Whaley's remaining gunners more experienced. The warrior might do that job himself tonight, but the Deacons weren't going to live and learn.

One of the Viets charged the door with his M-16 held at waist level. A sustained burst emptied the first magazine. Then he jumped aside as his comrade and Bolan crashed through the riddled door. It came off its hinges and flew down the hall, knocking a hardman off his feet.

He never got up. The Desert Eagle bucked in the Executioner's hands, and two bursts rattled from the Viet's M-16. Together they nailed the man to the bloody rug. They also alerted the men in the side rooms and upstairs.

A gunner leaped through the kitchen door, so close to Bolan that the warrior couldn't bring his .44 to bear. The Viets held their fire, afraid of hitting Bolan.

Fully loaded, the big Desert Eagle was about five pounds of metal. Bolan couldn't get off round, but he could swing. The five pounds slammed into the gunner's temple before he could raise his own weapon. He reeled against the frame of the kitchen door, stunned but still trying to draw.

Bolan had the .44 up and aimed when a Viet also saw a clear target. A line of 5.56 mm slugs stitched the man from throat to navel as he flew backward into the kitchen.

From in front and above, Bolan heard more shouting than shooting. He also heard a couple of familiar voices, one of them yelling, "Rackie, get your head down unless you've got your brains in your ass!"

Right now, meeting old friends was *not* good news. Mama Ruth's boys had showed up and stood a good chance of being blown away by Whaley's hardmen if Bolan didn't move fast.

Fast enough, probably, to get some of the White Tiger Viets killed. That was even worse news. Bolan understood all over again the saying "Save me from my friends and I can take care of my enemies."

The shooting started again in front, from both sides. Most of the Deacons were firing from the upper floor. Bolan listened and heard footsteps. The men on the ground floor were moving out to the side, both ways.

Flanking Mama Ruth's people, while the men above pinned them down? It made as much sense as anything else Whaley or Dawkins might have thought up. It also gave Bolan an opening, if he moved fast.

The Viets were now all in the kitchen, except for one on sentry at the back door. Bolan sent a second man to join the sentry and whispered his orders to the others.

They were ready to obey him. The treachery of one of their comrades hadn't paralyzed them with suspicion. Instead it had made them reckless with fury, determined to avenge this dishonor to the White Tigers and their people.

Phung nodded as Bolan finished his orders. The Vietnamese officer was nearly a foot shorter than Bolan, but his manner gave away nothing to the warrior. The Executioner knew that the Deacons were dead men, if Phung lived another ten minutes.

Right now they had maybe two of those ten minutes to strike before the Deacons butchered Mama Ruth's amateurs. Being the best at silent movement, Bolan took point. He also took the traitor's M-16 and flipped the selector to full-auto. This was room-cleaning time, not precision shooting.

Rifle held at waist level, Bolan flattened himself against the wall. His foot hooked out, yanking the hall door open, and he flipped a fragmentation grenade through the gap.

Somebody tried to throw the fragger back. His courage was wasted though, because the Executioner had kicked the door shut the moment the grenade vanished. It exploded in the next room. From the screams he knew it exploded in the face of the man who'd tried to throw it back.

Bolan tried to fling the door open, but the grenade had jammed it. He leveled the M-16, then remembered that light rounds on heavy wood could ricochet.

The Desert Eagle roared. The .44s chopped through the heavy wood, spitting dust and splinters. Someone behind the door shouted as it tottered and fell forward. Bolan jumped back, without swinging the muzzle of either weapon away from the doorway.

Which was what saved him. Two hardmen had survived the explosion, and they crouched behind a blood-spattered sofa, ignoring two bleeding, writhing comrades. One of them got off a wild burst from an Ingram, chipping plaster and hitting one of the Viets.

Bolan went into action at the same moment as the subgunner. So did three Viets. The air of the room was alive with flying lead. A .44 round from the Desert Eagle punched through the back of the sofa. A man behind it squealed like a stuck pig and toppled out from where he crouched.

Snaking low to the floor, the second survivor headed for the front hall. He got that far, before bullets slammed into the front door from the other side and into him. Mama Ruth's boys weren't using heavy stuff; he went down but kept moving. It took a burst from an M-16 to stop him.

That same burst alerted gunmen in the other half of the ground floor. Now it was the bad guys' turn to fill the room with bullets. If they calculated that their friends were either dead or expendable, it made sense.

The Executioner detected movement at the head of the stairs. Wondering what lay ahead, he settled the question by tossing one of his grenades. It was CS gas this time. If there were innocents in the house, they'd be upstairs or in the basement. Even if the people upstairs were gang members, they might become talkative prisoners.

The grenade popped in the middle of the shadowed movement. Somebody fired at Bolan, creased both him and a Viet, but gave both men a good target. Or at least one good enough. The man crashed down the stairs, assorted bullet holes drilled through his chest.

Bolan heard coughing, as well as shouting and shots from upstairs. He decided that there was no perfect time for storming the stairs, but now was good enough.

"Phung, the men out in front are friends. If they try anything, tell them that we thank Mama Ruth." Bolan pointed at two Viets. "Follow me."

They took the stairs in a rush, then went flat. Bolan pumped a burst from his 93-R into the only clear target, an arm that ended in a hand holding an automatic. The arm went limp, and the automatic clattered on the floor. Its owner screamed and fell into sight, where the Viets finished him off.

That alerted the rest of the people on the top floor, all two of them. They wouldn't have had much chance against Bolan alone. Against Bolan and the two Viets they were dead the moment they turned around. It just took them a few seconds to absorb enough lead to make the point.

There was more firing from the street. Bolan heard Phung shouting "We thank Mama Ruth!", which stopped some of the firing. The rest went on. It drew a scream from the roof, which ended in a crunching thud on the street below. Another lookout—or a desperate survivor trying to escape—had run out of luck.

Bolan decided that Mama Ruth's Jamaicans could almost be called professionals now. They might still have more enthusiasm than skill. But they carried guns, knew how to use them, and knew what they were fighting for. That was a fairly potent combination.

The Executioner and the Viets did a quick search of the top part of the house, the second floor and a low-ceilinged attic. They didn't find anybody else, living or dead, in the rooms. Bolan tossed a CS grenade into the attic to smoke out anyone either trying to hide or waiting in ambush. It drove out a few mice, a lot of cockroaches and nothing else.

It was now time to unite his forces and bring Mama Ruth's people up to date. Depending on when they started and where they started from, Whaley's reinforcements could be coming up the street any minute. That still might enable Bolan to carry out his plan of turning their trap against them.

A lot depended on the Jamaicans. Bolan stuck his head out the window and recognized Louis.

"Hey, Louis! Pollock here. Keep a lookout for Whaley's reinforcements."

Louis nodded. Bolan examined the bodies upstairs. None of them was Whaley, Dawkins or Calvin Pitts. Then he ran down the stairs two at a time.

He found the Jamaican friendlies and the Viets looking warily at one another, like two packs of wolves that didn't like each other's scent, but weren't sure whether that was enough reason to fight. Nobody had a weapon raised or a finger on a trigger.

The Executioner gave a one-minute briefing, then started assigning posts. "And one sniper on the roof," he concluded.

"Why not you?" Louis asked. "I get the feeling that's your specialty." He pointed at the Weatherby. "You don't haul that cannon around just for looks, do you?"

Bolan shook his head. As he started to reply, two cars hit the corner so fast that they took it on two wheels. Rubber squealed, then shrieked as the driver of the first car hit the brakes.

The second car hit the first, not hard enough to roll it, but both vehicles went over the edge of control.

The first car spun and slammed broadside into the rear of the friendly Jamaicans' van. The impact buckled and jammed the doors on the near side.

The second vehicle fishtailed wildly and finally rammed into a streetlight hard enough to cave in the whole front end. It wasn't hard enough to disable the men inside, who not only came out fast, but came out shooting, as well.

Bolan and Louis had been stepping forward, to order the men in the first car out and disarm them. Now Executioner, Jamaicans and Vietnamese all went hastily into reverse.

Fortunately the men from the second car were shooting high, to cover their friends without accidentally hitting them. They not only missed their friends, they missed their enemies, as well. The retreat of Bolan's force was a bit helter-skelter, but it was accomplished without casualties.

That shifted the balance in the fight decisively to Bolan's force. They were mostly under cover, half of them were trained soldiers and the soldiers had superior firepower and numbers.

Two of the men from the first car never reached the second. They were felled in the street, kicking in agony, then jerking as more bullets slammed into them. Phung finally had to punch one of his own men, who was preparing to riddle the dead all over again.

Bolan climbed onto the handiest roof that gave him a good sight line to the second car. He'd just finished reloading the Weatherby to capacity when the whole Deacon headquarters shuddered from roof to foundation. Most of the intact windows shattered, smoke rolled up from the bottom ones and chunks of siding and drainpipe peeled off and clattered into the street.

Then flames followed the smoke. The two friendlies who'd taken cover in the house dashed out steps ahead of the flames, one beating out a smoking patch on his trousers.

They ran right into the sights of the Deacons in the second car. But they were running fast, and the bad guys were too surprised at the explosion in the house to be aiming carefully. A dozen rounds went a dozen different ways, none of them hurting either of the running men.

The bullets did keep the other friendlies down. But in the process of shooting, the Deacons' reinforcements forgot about Bolan. Or maybe they'd never noticed him taking position.

In either case they exposed themselves so completely that Bolan suddenly had more targets than he could engage. He centered the cross hairs on the only man who seemed to have an assault rifle. A round blew the man's heart and lungs all over the hood of the car.

A second round started off aimed at a man's head. It actually hit his leg, as he dived into the car. Another hardman snatched up the discarded automatic weapon—it looked like a AR-15—and let several rounds fly in Bolan's general direction. Some of the slugs came close enough to make Bolan hold his fire.

He held it just long enough for the surviving Deacons to pile into the car. It made sense for them to be thinking of saving their own skins now. Wherever their boss was, he wasn't in the house. Not unless he was one of the corpses now about to be charred beyond recognition.

Flames were shooting out of the basement and ground-floor windows. Some of the second-floor windows were glowing as fire crept into the rooms behind them. The house, and all of Deacon Whaley's secrets that it held, would be rubble and ashes in a few more minutes.

The car backed away from the streetlight. Bolan waited until he had a clear shot at the driver, then took it. The window shattered. So did the driver's shoulder. His foot slammed down on the accelerator without taking the car out of reverse.

It shot backward across the street, rode up over the curb and slammed into a fire hydrant. The men in the back seat opened fire, but their wild bursts didn't keep the friendlies down this time.

Hundreds of rounds from M-16s and .38s sprayed the car and the men inside. Then, one of the Viets must have slipped in a magazine of tracer. A red line reached out, touched a leaking gasoline tank and caused a brief sunrise all along the street.

The blast nearly hurled Bolan off his perch. It took all of his strength to stay in place and not lose the Weatherby. He heard glass tinkle and crash up and down the street, and wondered if the explosion was just gasoline.

They'd never know what the car was carrying, or who had been in it. By the time the flames died out, you'd have been able to bury all the men together in a padded mailing envelope.

Bolan scrambled down from his perch. Over the roar of the flames he could hear sirens in the distance. The Jamaicans' van was a wreck; they would have to leave the area on foot, at least as far as his own van.

Nobody was hurt badly enough to need carrying, so their evacuation went off smoothly enough. Bolan's van was parked like a rush-hour subway car with men and weapons. But it could run, and it got them clear of the area before the police arrived.

If any more reinforcements for Deacon Whaley's now-defunct headquarters showed up, Bolan would leave them to the police. He himself had another concern.

He hadn't recognized Whaley, Dawkins, or Calvin Pitts among the bodies. Maybe they had crept down into the basement like the rats they were and died there.

Maybe, too, they had managed to escape while their people bought them time with blood. If the leaders were clean away and able to make contact with the survivors of the three gangs Deacon Whaley had ruled . . .

The man had to be run to ground or it had all been for nothing.

17

The watchman at the marina on the lower Potomac was Vietnamese but too young to remember much about the war or even about his native country. For him life really began when his parents brought him to America.

That life ended as a .45 round punched into his skull. Bigger Dawkins's big Star had a crude silencer and made no noise that anyone outside the marina could hear.

"Goin' to feel pretty silly, if it's stealin' this boat that gets the man on our tails," Deacon Whaley grumbled as he scrambled aboard the racing cruiser.

"We'd feel worse than silly if we went to our boat and found it staked out. Silly isn't dead, boss."

Adding the title was an afterthought to Calvin Pitts. If Whaley was letting Dawkins push him around, there wasn't much reason to be polite to the man.

There were quite a few reasons not to be, as a matter of act. Whaley's trap hadn't caught the big man. The big man had turned it on the Deacons, who were now going to end up as dead as the Kingdom and the Black Crabs. Unless Bigger Dawkins could figure out some way to save everybody the big man hadn't already wasted.

It struck Calvin Pitts that Dawkins had been real hot for the plan, too. Maybe Dawkins wasn't as smart as he thought he was. Or maybe he had some plans that would work better if there weren't so many Deacons around?

It didn't matter. Following Dawkins was Calvin Pitts's only alternative to staying on the dock until the police came and found him with the dead watchman. Then his ass would be either blown away or tossed in jail.

Pitts scrambled down into the boat. Dawkins was already at the controls, turning over the cruiser's two big diesels. He kept them throttled down as the boat backed out of the slip and into the river. Once he was in midchannel he opened the throttles.

The boat left a trail of white foam as it headed downstream, toward Chesapeake Bay and the open sea.

BOLAN WAS CHECKING HIMSELF for the kind of minor wounds that could cause major trouble if he ignored them, when the telephone rang. It was Hal Brognola.

"Striker, we've got a possible lead on where our friends went." Brognola went on to describe the theft of a racing cruiser from a downriver marina and the murder of the marina watchman.

"We might not have heard of it until morning," the head Fed added. "The police are running around in circles over your little firefight. The body count seems to have alarmed them."

"I was trying to alarm Deacon Whaley. Then add him to the body count."

"Well, a certain policewoman I think you've met decided that the boat theft after the firefight couldn't be coincidence. She didn't bother going through channels. She used our number right off."

Score another for Claire Brousson's level head. "Hal, we owe the lady one for this."

"Say no more. You want a lift down to the marina?"

"No. I want a lift out to *Peter Pan.*"

One of the advantages of working in the Washington area was that Stony Man Farm had a few unique local assets. One of these was a converted Swift boat named *Peter Pan.*

Based on the Eastern Shore, the boat spent most of her time testing exotic underwater detection and sabotage gear.

But the boat also retained her gun mounts and storage for a nice little arsenal below. Her two-man crew were both combat veterans. For chasing somebody down Chesapeake Bay and anywhere else between New York and Newport News, she was as good as they came.

"Okay. We don't have any classified gear aboard at the moment. Helicopter?"

"I wasn't expecting to walk."

"How many are you?"

Bolan did mental calculations. Phung, another Viet, and himself made three. Louis was the best of the Jamaican friendlies; he was also their leader. Could Mama Ruth's boys do without him for a few hours? Or maybe permanently, if the next firefight didn't go right?

Better than Bolan could do without Louis. The next best was Rackham, but with a chip on his shoulder, he might be too much of a burden. The other Jamaicans were unknown quantities. Bolan wasn't going to finish off this battle without letting at least one of Mama Ruth's people lend a hand. They'd paid their dues, for that much.

"Four. We'll rendezvous out in the bay. Call me back as soon as you have times and places."

"That's going to be pretty damned quick, Striker," Brognola replied. "As soon as I line things up for you, I have to call the Coast Guard. We need them."

"They'll be thrilled."

"Striker, the Coast Guard loves to haul in drug runners or people who help them. They've got half a dozen ships on their list of suspects, but no hard evidence against any of them. If we catch one of their suspects picking up Whaley, the Coast Guard will have them on a platter."

"In other words, take care of the shooting and leave the talking to you?"

"Well, a little specialization never hurt."

ONE OF THE RACING CRUISER'S engines coughed, then died.

"It sounds like a clogged fuel filter," Dawkins said. "I'll go and see if we have a spare."

It took Dawkins five minutes to find out that they didn't have a spare fuel filter, or a lot of other spare parts.

"I'm going to ask for my deposit back on this lemon," Dawkins said. His hands were black with grease and oil.

"If you get it, what you goin' to buy with it?" Whaley asked. To Calvin Pitts the boss's voice seemed dull, almost lifeless. He'd been sitting below, shoulders sagging, ever since they cleared the mouth of the Potomac.

"Another boat," Dawkins said. "One with two good engines. Plus a couple people to handle her, and play hostage until we meet up with your friends."

"What makes you think they're friends anymore?" Whaley said glumly. "We've messed up six ways from—"

"Not that bad, and not for good," Dawkins interrupted. He sounded as if he was trying to be soothing. "But even if it is that bad, will they like us talkin' to the Feds about the help they gave us?"

The ChiComs wouldn't like that one damned bit, Pitts knew. Beijing was real big on trying to maintain good relations with the West, to keep Western hardware flowing. They wouldn't be happy about the FBI or the CIA learning that Chinese weapons were letting American drug gangs play terrorist games on American soil. They would be incredibly unhappy.

"Calvin, you know the codes for reaching any Chinese ships offshore?" Dawkins asked.

"Boss?" Pitts looked at Whaley, who stared back. They both knew that if Whaley gave up the codes, it would be openly giving up leadership to Dawkins. They also both knew the alternative.

"Get me a pad and some paper," Whaley grumbled. "They didn't give me anythin' for fancy messages, though. We'll just have to hope."

"I'm also going to throttle back the one engine we've got until we see a boat we can borrow,"

Dawkins said. "We can't do much chasing, but I'm betting we'll have to do some."

BOLAN SQUATTED on the skids of the Bell JetRanger until Louis was clear. Then he leaped, landing in a five-point roll on *Peter Pan*'s aluminum deck.

Without rising, the Executioner waved to the helicopter pilot. The chopper banked slightly and buzzed away, keeping low until it was over land. With the haze on the bay that morning, nobody was likely to see the rendezvous with the boat.

When the helicopter was out of sight, Bolan went below to check his equipment. The boat's captain met him, his tanned face set in a grim mask.

"We got a problem, Mr. Pollock."

"The boat or the mission?"

"Boat's fine. The mission may be screwed."

"Let's have it."

The stolen racer had been sighted drifting in the bay. A sports fisherman with three passengers and two crew had also missed her regular CB radio report a half hour before the sighting. At the time of the report the sports fisherman would have been within a mile or two of where the stolen boat was later found.

"So our friends left a trail but we can't follow it?"

"Hostages puts a whole new face on things, doesn't it?"

"Not necessarily." Bolan looked at the chart. "Let's start down the bay anyway."

"But we can't endanger—"

"We won't be endangering anybody. All we'll be doing is putting ourselves where we can take advantage of any mistakes our friends make."

"And if they don't make any?" The captain sounded as if he wanted to be optimistic but had seen too many good plans produce bad outcomes.

"We put the squeeze on them until they do."

The other man nodded reluctantly and went on deck. Bolan made a mental note. If the fighting started, he would rely more on the second crewman, an ex-Seal.

HAL BROGNOLA HAD more than once read the riot act to four-star generals. So he had no problem talking with a Coast Guard rear admiral who was willing to cooperate.

Not that the rear admiral had all that much choice, as Brognola had politely reminded him early in the conversation.

"We've got the equivalent of a good SWAT team already afloat and in pursuit. You don't even *have* a SWAT team."

"We're working on it."

"Fast enough to have it in place by lunchtime?" Brognola pressed.

"You put it that way, no."

The admiral had admitted that the Coast Guard needed any assets Stony Man Farm was prepared to provide. Now he was trying to get Brognola to admit that the man he had in place, one Rance Pollock, needed the Coast Guard as badly as it needed him.

"You've got one boat with limited electronics, and no aircraft at all. We've got plenty of both, all with radar up the wazoo."

"Did I say I doubted that?"

"You're doing a pretty good imitation of a man who either doesn't need us or doesn't want to admit it."

"Actually, I'm a man who wants to divide up this fight, so our people don't wind up tripping over each other."

"Or shooting at each other by mistake," the admiral added. "Another reason I want to wind this up fast. We go chasing around out there after dark, with nothing but radar and IR signatures to go on, and the wrong people could get blown away."

Brognola made a mental note to pull the admiral's personal data. He was pleasantly combat-oriented.

"We've got four ships on our list of possible contacts for your friends," the admiral continued.

"I know." Brognola rattled off the names. The silence on the line lasted a long time.

When the admiral came back, he sounded torn between anger and embarrassment. "Who told you?"

"Ah, Admiral, you don't have a need to know."

"About a penetration of our own data base?"

"Put it that way, you have a point." Brognola himself didn't always know how Aaron Kurtzman and his experts managed their raids on other people's data. He sometimes suspected that it was better that way.

"Let's cut a deal, Admiral. You throw in all the assets you can spare to keep our boat and its target under surveillance. You also keep an eye out for any of the ships on the suspect list. If one of them so much as flushes her bilges at the wrong time, we want to know and we want our people to know.

"In return we give you the credit for any hostage rescues. We also give you a crash course in computer security."

"Is anybody else as good as you people are?"

Brognola managed to laugh. "I'd like to pay for that compliment by saying no way. But there are hackers out there as good as anybody we have. There's also enough drug money to buy them."

"Tell me about it," the admiral said wearily. "Okay, we'll be scrambling air and sea assets as fast as we can. The cover story will be a distress message from a yacht. I'll call back in about an hour with a list of what we'll have."

"Thanks, Admiral."

Brognola was sincere. The Executioner was the best there was, no doubt about it. He could be even better when he didn't have to watch his back.

18

Aboard a forty-eight foot sports fisherman, Calvin Pitts clung to the tuna tower. He tried to scan the hazy horizon with a pair of barely focused binoculars. He also tried not to think about being seasick. The sea was calm, but being up on the tower exaggerated what rolling there was. Also, Pitts was at home on dry land.

Dawkins stepped out of the pilothouse and waved to Pitts. "Anything on the radio?"

"Coasties say they've got a yacht in trouble. Everybody's to keep an eye open."

"Any description?"

"Not yet."

Then it might be real, and the Coast Guard wasn't on their trail.

"Anything in sight?" Dawkins asked.

"Nobody doin' anything I'd worry about," Pitts replied. "Hard to see with this haze."

Dawkins scrambled up the ladder to join Pitts, borrowed the binoculars and made his own study of the horizon. Finally he handed them back and nodded.

"You might make a sailor yet."

"Who's got an eye on our friends?"

"Deacon. But don't sweat it. I tied up the captain ten minutes ago. Put him down with the other four. Looked like he might be wonderin' about our leavin' them alive."

"What—"

Dawkins jerked a thumb over the side. "Soon as we meet our friends, anyway. Need them until then, just in case the Coasties show up and want to shoot."

"Are we going to meet those friends?" An hour ago Whaley said he'd raised what he thought was one of the contact ships. He wasn't sure, and the ship hadn't given a rendezvous.

Pitts didn't like the situation, but he knew he liked the fate waiting for him on land even less. He clapped the binoculars back to his eyes and started to examine the horizon again. He wanted to spot anything larger than a shark's fin before it spotted him.

THE TURBOCHARGED DIESELS of the *Peter Pan* drove the vessel effortlessly through the gentle swell at a steady twenty-five knots. In the pilothouse Bolan finished a final adjustment to the sights of the Weatherby, then cleaned the lenses. Salt air and haze made a bad combination for long-range shooting.

Colonel Phung watched Bolan intently, ignoring the boat's mate at the wheel. When he saw that the Executioner was finished with the Weatherby, he pointed outside. The warrior nodded and followed.

"What if we don't find them?" Phung asked.

The bow thumped through a higher swell and spray fountained over both men. Bolan wiped salt off his face before replying.

"Today or at all?"

"If we do not find them today, can my people and I count on your help in finding them wherever they go?"

Bolan considered what Phung was implying. They wanted help—his and Stony Man's—in tracking down the enemies who had dishonored them. Phung could forgive being put in danger; he was a soldier. He couldn't forgive somebody who had turned one of his trusted soldiers into a traitor.

He was afraid that the CIA would tell him to forget it. But Phung would not, and if the Company wouldn't help him pursue what they would no doubt call a private vendetta, he wanted Bolan's help.

The Executioner didn't want to ask what Phung might offer in return. Any hint of bargaining would insult the proud little colonel.

Besides, Bolan really couldn't see what Phung had to offer. The CIA would hit the ceiling if the White Tiger Society's covert-operations people went over to Stony Man Farm, who in turn really didn't need a couple of dozen stubborn and dedicated Vietnamese, anyway. The question was what Mack Bolan needed to do to be true to his own standards.

The answer was simple. If Phung asked for Bolan's help, he would get it. He owed Phung that much.

He also owed it to Hal Brognola not to involve Stony Man Farm. The warrior had worked free-lance before and could do so again. If he helped Phung, he could be completely deniable. And if he helped Phung, any of the fleeing drug lords who survived today wouldn't survive the next meeting.

"If there's anyone to go after tomorrow, I'll go with you," Bolan said.

They shook hands. Then both turned toward the screen in front of the wheel where the vessel's high-powered radar was sketching the sea around them.

"WE GOT A REPLY," Whaley said. For the first time in days he looked cheerful.

"Firm?" Dawkins asked.

"It's Contact Point 28. They have the right codes, and they told me they're comin' in."

"ETA?"

"Couple hours at least. They want us a little bit offshore, in case the Coasties or the Navy gets snoopy."

"Don't blame them at all." Bigger Dawkins yawned. "If all our friends are tied up nice and tight, anybody mind if I put my feet up? Running for your life takes it out of a man."

"Let me go down and check the ropes," Pitts suggested. There was something in Dawkins's face and voice, something that he saw but Whaley apparently didn't. When whatever it was came down, Pitts didn't want to have his back turned to Dawkins.

Pitts scrambled down from the pilothouse into the cabin, where the three fishermen and two crew were laid out on the deck like rolled-up rugs. None of them looked too happy, but none of them looked too far gone either. They were dead men, of course, but there was a time and a place for them to die. Luckily for them it wasn't yet.

Pitts had knelt to check the captain's bindings when he heard the shot. His 10 mm gun was in his hand before he stood up. He faced the hatch and shouted, "Hey, what's going on?"

A gurgle answered him, then a second shot. Pitts backed away, until he was crouching in the doorway to the forward cabin, his gun aimed at the pilothouse.

"I said what's going on?"

A thump, and Deacon Whaley sprawled into view. His eyes were open but blank, and his chest was one big smear of blood.

Bigger Dawkins followed Whaley. Dawkins was on his feet, the Star .45 in his hand until he saw the look on Calvin Pitts's face. Then he let the automatic drop to his side, muzzle aimed at the deck.

"Calvin, you got to understand. Deacon would have cut us out with the Chinese. I've had enough of that, and I think you have, too. It was either him or us, once we'd made contact."

Calvin Pitts understood that Dawkins was telling the truth. He also knew that Dawkins wouldn't have ruled out finishing off Pitts, if that meant covering his tracks a little better.

"What are you offerin' the ChiComs, without Deacon?"

"New York action, man. I've got a whole gang back there that needs a boss and a good top gun. We trade with the ChiComs—they give us the gang, the gang gives them what they need in New York."

"So you're sayin' Whaley was dead, but he wouldn't lie down?"

"Right. I had to take care of that."

"You did." Pitts leathered his weapon. "Okay, Mr. Dawkins. I can live without Deacon. Really truly I can. But you'd better not decide you can live without me."

"I might say the same thing," Dawkins said.

"Then we can get along real well," Pitts concluded. At least for the next couple of hours, he added to himself.

BOLAN WAS BELOW when the Coast Guard came on the radio, doing limbering-up exercises when the mate shouted down from the pilothouse.

"Incoming call for Striker."

Bolan's legs shot him up the ladder to the radio, where he snatched up the headset and mike.

"Angler Four to Striker," he heard. "We have a double contact. Objects one and two, on converging courses. Estimated time of contact, eighty minutes. Object one is twenty-one thousand yards from your position, bearing one-forty-five true, speed sixteen knots, course one hundred true."

A computerized map display showed the relative positions of object one—the sports fisherman—and object two—one of the suspicious ships. Bolan punched in the position of his own vessel.

"Can we catch them before they rendezvous with the other ship?" he asked.

The captain looked at the display and shrugged. "Yes, if we step on the gas. We'll show up on their radar, though. I thought we wanted to be sneaky."

"We do," Bolan said. Alerting Whaley and friends too soon could be a death sentence for the hostages. The ship heading for them might also have more firepower than *Peter Pan* could face.

Bolan looked at the display again, then said, "Striker to Angel Four. We have a problem with object one. Can you slow up two a bit?" Without communications security he couldn't give detailed suggestions, although he had several ideas. If the Coast Guard pilot was worth half his salary, he'd have the same ones. If he didn't, he'd be able to get them over a secure channel from an admiral instructed by Hal Brognola.

"Angel Four to Striker. Give me five minutes. I need to talk to Angel Two."

Angel Two was the Coast Guard cutter *Point Lompas.* She was part of the surface support for Operation Angel, she and the ex-cocaine runner speedout she was towing.

The conversation with Angel Two was on a different wavelength, but it went faster than predicted.

In two minutes Bolan heard "We have a roger from Angel Two. She has objects on her radar and will execute as directed."

"Thanks, Angel Two. We'll cover any unauthorized material expenditures."

"Buy the beer if we bring this off, and we'll call it square."

"You're on, Angel Two. Striker out."

Both crewmen were looking at Bolan. So were Colonel Phung and Louis. The remaining Viet, Corporal Tho, was below loading magazines.

"We've got a clear shot at our friends, without any of *their* friends butting in," Bolan said.

"Shall I mount the M-60?" the mate asked, grinning.

"Load and lock, but don't mount it," Bolan replied. "That sports fisherman probably doesn't have the greatest radar in the world. Even at top speed it won't be able to make us as armed. But if we come zooming up with an MG sticking out..."

"I get the picture." The captain sounded relieved.

THE TRAWLER HAD STARTED life in a Polish shipyard and served nine years in the Soviet navy. Then, as a cheap gesture of friendship, she'd been sold to the North Koreans. After that her odyssey would have filled a novel.

She was now traveling the Russian papers again, even though she was actually a unit of the Chinese People's Liberation Navy. Her crew were all Russian-speaking Chinese, pretending to be Siberians or Mongolians. She wore the name *Golden Eye*, and her job was to support covert operations off the American coast and spy on Russian spy ships.

This second mission was, in her captain's opinion, the more important of the two. Neither the Chinese or any of her friends could do anything militarily significant on the Eastern Seaboard of the United States. But learning what the Russians knew about American air, sea, and space operations was valuable.

The goodwill of countries who received that information was even more so. Since the fall of communism in the former Soviet republics, it became necessary—and profitable—for someone to fill the intelligence void. If the People's Republic could rise to the occasion, so much the better.

Her captain thought her name, *Golden Eye*, very appropriate. She was an eye that saw much, and what she saw was worth more than gold.

Certainly she wasn't an eye to be closed on a whim, which seemed to be what the political officer wanted. The captain recognized the signs of frustration in the man already. Soon he would see rage, and finally hear an explosion of temper.

"We must make the rendezvous!" the political officer shouted. "The people aboard are critical to future operations in America."

"Not as critical as the continued operation of this ship," the captain replied in what he hoped was a soothing tone.

"How can we put ourselves in danger by making the rendezvous?"

"The Coast Guard informs us that we are the nearest surface vessel to survivors from the sunken yacht."

"There is no—"

"I beg your pardon, Comrade, but I cannot read the minds of the Americans. They may be lying. They may also be telling the truth. If they are telling the truth, we could be refusing to go to the aid of persons in danger at sea.

"The Coast Guard disapproves of this strongly," the captain went on. He thought that if he ever made a bigger understatement, it should be put on a bronze plaque in Shanghai. "They will investigate. They may even request permission to board us."

"We will refuse."

"Then they may declare that we are suspected of smuggling drugs, obtain a warrant and come aboard anyway. Or, they may simply give our name and description to the navies of other nations. The Americans are not the only people whose curiosity we need to fear."

The political officer's reply was lost in the roar of a large airplane passing low overhead. Looking up, the captain saw an American C-130 Hercules with Coast

Guard markings fading into the haze. A moment later the radio operator called.

"Comrade Captain, the Americans are calling again. They say they do not have rescue swimmers aboard, but are dropping a life raft to the survivors. They will also drop a smoke float on their next pass."

Why the Americans couldn't drop both at once was a mystery to the captain. He couldn't help wondering if the political officer was right about being tricked.

He also couldn't help knowing that he'd spoken the truth, when he said *Golden Eye* could never directly disobey a Coast Guard request. But it might be possible to obey the Coast Guard without abandoning their friends.

He called the deputy captain. "Comrade Lin. I want four volunteers to take the boat to rendezvous with an American vessel." He described the sports fisherman.

"Ah, yes, Comrade Captain," Lin replied. "Small arms only?"

"If anything larger can be concealed . . ."

"Of course. Also, I think they shall go in civilian clothes and carry fishing gear. If they are sighted, we can say they were going fishing to supplement our rations."

"Excellent, Comrade Lin. Have the men and boat ready in fifteen minutes. By then we should be in the middle of that patch of fog." He pointed off to starboard. "It looks thick enough to hide us not only from sea level but from the air."

The political officer was smiling, but looking confused. "How will our men find their way to meet the Americans?"

The captain looked at him almost pityingly. He could afford a sense of superiority now. "Our radar is the finest the People's Republic has put aboard a ship. We shall track the Americans as we head for the 'survivors,' then guide our boat by radio."

"If the Americans intercept our messages—"

"We will use code and burst transmission. They may hear, but they will hardly understand."

19

The sports fisherman's motion changed as Bigger Dawkins cut back the throttles. The engines' roar died to a mutter, then faded into silence.

With no manmade noises, the sheer size of the ocean hit Calvin Pitts like a blow. He'd be glad to get aboard something bigger than this fishing boat, happier still to be on dry land. As for taking a job that meant working afloat, he'd almost rather take his chances with the police.

"Shall I dump our friends below?" Pitts asked.

Dawkins shook his head. "Not yet. Somebody besides our friends could still show up."

"Are the Chinese *swimming?*"

Dawkins looked over the side. "If they do, they're in bad trouble. I get the feeling there's sharks out."

"Sweet."

Pitts considered going below to at least dump Whaley's body, but decided after a moment that it wouldn't help. He couldn't wipe up the blood in time.

The fog seemed to have thickened since Dawkins cut the engines. Or had Dawkins just stopped them in the middle of a good patch? Anyway, it was hard to see more than twice the length of the boat in any direction.

Pitts could hear, though. He heard the splash of water against the hull, the distant cries of seabirds and something else too distant to identify. It sounded manmade, and Pitts concentrated all his attention on identifying it. After a minute he thought he had it.

It didn't make a lot of sense to hear an outboard motor this far out in the Atlantic. But if the last twenty-four hours had made sense, Pitts knew he wouldn't be this far out in the Atlantic in the first place.

THE EXECUTIONER'S final approach to the sports fisherman was based on three assumptions.

Whaley's men had no way of detecting *Peter Pan*'s radar.

The Chinese—it had to be them—aboard object two did, but not if it wasn't aimed at them. If *Peter Pan* concentrated on the sports fisherman and left the Chinese to the Coast Guard, all would be well—or at least better.

Finally, if *Peter Pan* made her final approach silently, neither Whaley nor the Chinese would hear her. The Chinese probably had somebody on passive sonar, listening for mysterious noises. They might hear one, all right, but it would stay mysterious until it was too late.

"Any problem with any of this?" Bolan asked the captain.

"You're kind of guessing about what the ChiComs have and don't have," the captain observed.

"We are," Phung stated. "But it is foolish in war to assume that your enemy is strong at all points. That's the same as lying down and letting yourself be defeated before you have fought. The secret of victory is to guess your opponent's weak points and attack them.''

The mate grinned. Bolan guessed that the ex-SEAL had wanted to say pretty much the same, but had kept quiet out of respect for a superior.

''Well, your asses are even farther out on the line than mine,'' the captain said. ''Let's go. Rig for silent running and bring the M-60 up into the pilothouse. When you hear 'Man deck guns!' I want that mother firing before I finish the order.''

''Aye, aye, captain,'' the mate said.

Peter Pan slowed down, and the rumble of her engines faded into silence for a moment as the captain shifted the exhausts to the underwater outlets. Then she began picking up speed again, until she was moving at ten knots through haze that grew thicker every few hundred yards.

In the pilothouse Bolan again counted the rounds for the Weatherby in his blacksuit pocket and stared at the radar screen. Unless the Coast Guard was half-blind, their target was barely a mile ahead.

Bolan had some experience with reading radar screens. But he wasn't a trained radar operator, so it was no surprise that he missed an extra blip. The blip was about the size you would have expected from a small boat, and was approaching the target from the opposite direction of the vessel.

''COMRADE CAPTAIN, radar reports that another vessel is approaching our friends from the opposite side,'' Deputy Lin reported.

''Is it transmitting anything?''

"No, and it is moving slowly. Sonar thinks they hear slow-speed propellers at about the right distance."

"Probably a private yacht. Tell our comrades in the gig to be careful to avoid collision, and not to open fire unless fired upon." The captain winced at the mere thought of the consequences of shooting up an American yacht.

"Yes, Comrade Captain."

BOLAN STOOD on the forecastle with the Desert Eagle and the Beretta concealed by the windbreaker he wore over the blacksuit. The Weatherby and CS grenades lay in a locker, a foot from Bolan's hand.

He looked formidable but unarmed, nothing surprising to see standing lookout aboard a boat groping her way through this kind of haze.

What one couldn't see was that he could be armed and in action within five seconds.

The vessel's bow lifted on a swell, then thumped down. As the thump died away, Bolan thought he saw a more solid patch ahead in the haze.

"I think I have a visual on our target," he said softly.

The intercom was silent for a moment. Then Phung said, "Come on deck?"

"Yes, but stay down. Louis, Tho, you back up the M-60."

"Mr. Pollock, you want to hog all the fun," Louis grumbled.

"You mean you still think people shooting at you is—" Then Bolan broke off. The fog distorted sound and made it hard to tell directions, but he'd certainly heard an outboard motor nearby.

THE PETTY OFFICER commanding the gig was an atheist, so he didn't thank God for the sports fisherman's tuna tower. It rose just high enough to enable him to find the boat under it.

With that fix he could maneuver around to the other side of the American craft. He didn't entirely believe his captain's assurances that the other craft must be friendly. It was probably, but he wanted to be between it, and the sports fisherman before he picked up the agents. If he was wrong, he would lose nothing but a little time.

If he was right, he could save the whole mission—he and the machine gun lying on the bottom of the gig under a canvas cover. He would also be saving his own life, which either the Americans or his own people might end if the mission failed. He had never heard of a captain accepting blame for a failure, when there was a petty officer to accuse.

PETER PAN WAS NOW RUNNING dead slow. She was also swinging gently to starboard, ready to come alongside the sports fisherman bow to stern.

They had the missing boat in front of them, no doubt about it. The worst thing that could happen was that the boat had gone missing for innocent reasons. That was why Bolan was going to give Whaley and company the first shot. A bullet aimed at you was positive ID enough.

Peter Pan finished her turn, then the deck quivered as the engines went into reverse. Slowly she backed toward the sports fisherman.

Bolan crouched, hands ready to draw his weapons. He watched the pilothouse of the sport fisherman, saw one dark face there and thought he saw another peering down from the tuna tower.

Then the outboard motor roared from aft, and a shot from the tuna tower sank into the locker beside the Executioner.

CALVIN PITTS, the landlubber, kept a better lookout than the professionals aboard *Peter Pan*.

He was the first to see the Chinese gig glide out of the mist and head for the sports fisherman's stern. He snapped off the safety on his weapon and peered at the other boat ahead.

It looked as if it might be official. It certainly had a lot of radar gear, but no guns and no markings. If the Chinese played it cool, he would do the same. Enough cool to go around, and maybe the new visitors wouldn't get suspicious.

If they did, there were always the hostages below. Pitts was glad he'd taken Dawkins's advice not to ditch them.

Then he saw the lookout on the new boat's bow, clearly enough to recognize. Pitts's finger took on a life of its own and squeezed the trigger.

IF PITTS BARELY KNEW what he was doing in the first moments of the firefight, nobody else knew even that much.

Bolan dived for cover, popping the locker hatch as he did. At this range the Desert Eagle would do the job, but the Weatherby would be needed before the shooting ended.

Aft, the Chinese hesitated just long enough to give the mate a head start on mounting the M-60. That was crucial, because the ChiCom's MG didn't need to be mounted. The petty officer snatched off the canvas cover, the gunner hoisted the weapon in his arms and he opened fire the moment the muzzle bore vaguely on target.

Both machine guns went into action at the same time, too quickly to be accurate even at nearly point-blank range. The M-60's bursts went into the water astern of the Chinese boat. The Chinese rounds sprayed the pilothouse, knocking out a lot of glass and a few instruments but not hurting anyone.

This gave both Bigger Dawkins and Calvin Pitts a few undistracted moments to deal with Mack Bolan. They needed more than time; they needed heavier firepower. They also didn't need to be diverted by Colonel Phung as they drew down.

Phung burst onto *Peter Pan*'s forecastle and went down so hard that Bolan thought he'd been hit. He'd only tripped over a coil of mooring line. Phung still had his M-16 in hand and rolled, swinging up the muzzle as he poured out a magazine on full automatic.

With all those rounds he had to have hit something besides the sport fisherman's pilothouse windows. But he didn't hit Bigger Dawkins, who couldn't resist a better target than the Executioner.

Phung's body jerked as two .45 rounds tore into it.

In the next few seconds Bolan forgot about the Weatherby, Phung and everything else except his chance to get aboard the sports fisherman. If he did, he could get between the hostages below and anyone after them.

The Executioner sprang across the narrow gap of water. A roll saved him from fractures, if not from bruises. Another roll saved him from two 10 mm rounds.

Pitts might have scored with his third, but the Executioner was moving fast. The Jamaican also made a serious mistake. He not only let himself rely too much on his friends, he let them distract him.

The Chinese had grenades, and a sailor tossed two of them aboard *Peter Pan*. The mate tossed one back, and it erupted in the water like a baby depth charge. The second one landed just out of reach.

With no time to do anything else, the mate abandoned his gun and dived onto the grenade. He had it clamped tightly against his weightlifter's torso when it exploded.

The captain saw the explosion, watched his mate and friend being dismembered and had the Chinese who'd done it in the sights of his Beretta. The grenade thrower died in the next moment, and the petty officer fell overboard seconds later.

The third and fourth Chinese went different ways. One of them was the machine gunner, who swept the muzzle back and forth, hitting the captain but missing Louis and Tho. Because the gunner had both 5.56 mm rounds and .38 Specials in him when they did the autopsy, it was hard to tell whether Louis or Tho hit him first. Both certainly hit him hard.

The last Chinese leaped aboard the sports fisherman, a rescuer needing rescue. He landed behind Bigger Dawkins, who whirled like a dervish.

Dawkins stopped himself short of wasting the Chinese sailor. But he turned his back on the door to the cabin just as the Executioner reached it.

The Desert Eagle roared. Dawkins took one Magnum round in the chest, another in the throat. He hit the Chinese sailor behind him hard enough to knock the man's rifle out of his hand.

The sailor didn't waste time trying to retrieve it. With a wild yell he flung himself over the stern of the sports fisherman into the gig. A moment later the outboard motor coughed to life.

Something splashed alongside, then it or something else bumped the side of the boat. Bolan glimpsed what he thought might be blood in the water. Then spray erupted, as if another grenade had exploded.

Out of the spray rose Calvin Pitts's head. He'd jumped from the tuna tower, done a bellyflopper, but survived. Now he was swimming desperately after the Chinese boat.

Bolan sighed on Pitts's head. As the warrior's finger tightened on the trigger, the head suddenly vanished. Then it popped to the surface again, mouth gaping. The warrior heard Pitts screaming.

The Jamaican rose half out of the water, still screaming. The Executioner glimpsed a gray fin just behind him. Then fin and head both vanished, and the scream died as the shark took Calvin Pitts down into the depths of the sea.

The Chinese boat was out of pistol range, but Tho still had his M-16. That was enough, as a sudden orange flare in the haze told Bolan. Tracer bullets in the gasoline tank had finished the gig as efficiently as anyone could wish.

Bolan cupped his hands and shouted, "Hey! Is anybody in shape to go after our Chinese friend before the sharks get him?"

A battered Louis pulled himself to his feet. "Captain's hurt, mate's dead, Tho and I can't run the boat and I think Phung's down."

Bolan pulled out the sports fisherman's life raft, popped its inflater cartridge and dropped it over the side.

By the time he'd paddled back to *Peter Pan*, the captain was in shape to at least see if the boat would run. Colonel Phung was dying.

He managed a faint smile as Bolan knelt beside him. "Is there a trail to follow? If so, I am sorry I will not be with you on it."

"No need to apologize. Any soldier can have bad luck. And this fight's over."

"Not quite. Those Chinese—the ship that sent them—" Blood trickled from Phung's mouth, and the hand gripping Bolan's fell back on the deck.

A moment later screams in the haze told the warrior that the last surviving Chinese would lead them nowhere. Blood in the water had led the sharks to him first.

That wouldn't have annoyed Bolan so much, if he hadn't discovered that neither of the two boats had a single functioning radio.

"I'll get the survival beacon from the life raft," Bolan said. "Maybe we can raise the Coast Guard with that. Then I'll stay on the M-60.

"Louis, you know first-aid?"

"Some."

Bolan gave a two-minute lecture on how to help men who'd been bound hand and foot for most of a day. "You go untie the hostages and hold the fort aboard the fisherman until they're on their feet. Tho, you ride shotgun."

"This is not—" the Viet said, hefting his M-16.

The captain saw Bolan's frown and diverted him with a cough. "Yeah, okay, and maybe somebody'd better lash the boats together, too. Otherwise there's going to be lots of water and sharks between us before the Coast Guard arrives."

"If they do," Louis said glumly.

LOUIS'S VOTE of no confidence in the Coast Guard turned out to be pessimistic.

The survival beacon produced an airdrop of rescue swimmers, in spite of the sharks, one of them a paramedic loaded with first-aid supplies. With able-bodied boathandlers aboard, *Peter Pan* was able to get under way, towing the sports fisherman.

HALF AN HOUR LATER, the first of the hostages was fit to take the sports fisherman's wheel. They cast off the tow line, and the two boats headed for shore at a steady fifteen knots.

With a new radio tuned to Coast Guard frequencies they followed the last act of the day's drama. But they didn't experience it as the captain of *Golden Eye* did.

The captain had a fairly good idea of what had happened from his radar and the long silence that followed the battle. He had no idea how much the Americans might know. If they didn't know enough, behaving like an innocent man might actually make them think he was one.

He was quartering the area of the "survivors" methodically for the third time, when a Coast Guard cutter approached at full speed. It was the *Point Lomas,* with a request to heave to and prepare to be boarded. The radar reported a second and larger vessel standing off about fifteen thousand yards.

"The radar signature is that of a Hamilton-class cutter," the operator reported. "I detect them scanning us with their own radar."

"All hands!" the captain called. "All hands, prepare to abandon ship! This is not a drill. I repeat, all hands prepare to abandon ship!"

For a moment the political officer was too astonished to speak. Then he ran toward a group of sailors who were already peeling the cover off one of the lifeboats.

"I forbid obedience to this cowardly order," he shouted. "Stop that at once. We will remain on board and defy the Americans!"

The captain drew his pistol. "If you wish to remain on board, Comrade, that can be arranged." Then he shot the man through the head. As the political officer collapsed, Deputy Captain Lin came on deck.

"Please take care of the men, and make sure that they do not dishonor themselves or the navy while in American hands."

Lin stared briefly, saw no answer in his friend's face, then nodded and started shouting orders. The captain went below, waited ten minutes, then set the fuses for the scuttling charges.

Golden Eye's captain had both bad luck and good luck. His bad luck was that the explosives in the scuttling charges had deteriorated since they were installed. They only sprang a few plates, instead of blowing gaping holes in the ship's hull, which would have sent her to the bottom in a few minutes.

She was still afloat when the American boarding party scrambled up her side. They had a busy few minutes making sure she would stay afloat, but they succeeded.

The captain never knew of his failure. The explosions scattered fragments around the engine room. One of them pierced his skull, and he was dying when the Americans found him. He died aboard the cutter *Jarvis* before the helicopter, dispatched to transport him to Bethesda Naval Hospital, reached the ship.

Instead, the helicopter was diverted to the little convoy of *Peter Pan* and the sports fisherman. One helicopter had already taken off the wounded. This one took off the bodies and Mack Bolan, for a proper debriefing.

The two Coast Guardsmen finished bringing the boats home.

EPILOGUE

"So the CIA forgives us for getting Phung killed?"

"They didn't start off wanting to," Brognola told Bolan. "But I made a few telephone calls. Besides, we handed the Pentagon a real live Chinese intelligence trawler. We now have friends in military high places."

"What a relief," Bolan said dryly. "I wish we knew who took out our Vietnamese traitor."

The traitor and Chuyen's body had been swept up by the D.C. police when they descended on what was left of Whaley's headquarters. Before Stony Man could trace and claim the traitor, he had been found hanged in his cell in the D.C. jail. "Suicide" was the verdict; "murder to silence a witness" was the probable truth.

" 'If wishes were fishes...' " Brognola quoted.

"True. And there are probably cutouts all along the line, so even if the police took it seriously they might not get anywhere."

"If it's any consolation, Striker, I'm going to have a word with the D.C. police. We won't blow the whistle on them for losing a prisoner in a nationally important case. On the other hand they don't pull in any of our Viets on anything worse than a drunk-driving charge without telling us."

"Hal, are you sure you wouldn't rather play the stock market? You've got a nice talent for hard bargaining?"

"Light pockets make for easy consciences, I've found. Anything else?"

"No. I'll be out of touch for a few hours. Claire Brousson has offered to cook me dinner tonight."

"Cementing police-community relations?"

"Hal, I seriously doubt if that young lady has ever needed to use cement. Good night."

Brognola set the receiver back in its cradle. A messy case was over, as much as anyone could reasonably expect, and the victor was enjoying...

No, the big Fed couldn't call dinner with Claire Brousson "the spoils." Call it a little bit of the civilization Mack Bolan had sworn to defend, against the barbarians who would tear it down.

A Western crime alliance
threatens Russia's new freedom

DON PENDLETON's

MACK BOLAN ®

ONSLAUGHT

The Brotherhood—an alliance between a North
American Mafia family and a South American drug
cartel—could spell doom for a newly free Russia.
Fearing that a sudden crime wave might shift the
balance of power back to Communism, the U.S.
President sends in the man who represents ultimate
justice, within or beyond the law. Only the Executioner
can deliver.

Omega Force is caught dead center in a brutal Middle East war
in the next episode of

by PATRICK F. ROGERS

In Book 2: **ZERO HOUR,** the Omega Force is dispatched on a
search-and-destroy mission to eliminate enemies of the U.S.
seeking revenge for Iraq's defeat in the Gulf—enemies who will
use any means necessary to trigger a full-scale war.

With capabilities unmatched by any other paramilitary organization in the world, Omega Force is a special ready-reaction anti-
terrorist strike force composed of the best commandos and
equipment the military has to offer.